RIDE
IN THE
OPEN SPACES

John W. Hayes

Ride in the Open Spaces

Phil 4:13 - *I can do all things through Christ who strengthens me.*

ISBN   978-0-9793399-2-9   (paperback)
ISBN   978-0-9793399-3-6   (e-book)

Publisher:
Hunting Through History
38110 County Road 469
Cohasset, MN 55721
www.huntingthroughhistory.com

Printed in the United States of America

Credits:
 Front Cover: photo courtesy Mark Sage,
   Mike Brown photographer
 Back Cover: photo by Ric Lambert, used with permission,
   art by John W. Hayes

Table of Contents

Ride in the Open Spaces

I wish to thank the readers/editors, my daughter Johannah
and my wife Connie for their assistance and support.

Review

If you like horses, history, and learning about North Dakota, you
need to read "Ride in the Open Spaces." Follow Cantry and Jewel
on their quest to find missing cattle, that were spooked by wild
dogs. They will need to use their knowledge of the land to track the
animals. Along the way they will discuss Cantry's new found passion of rendezvous and what it means to really understand history.
As things get late into the day the duo will get a chance to make
camp with some friends and discuss the true purposes of rendezvous. **@a_classy_rebel_reader**

Other books by the Author

Seven Thought Provoking Essays on the Subject of Participating in
Historical Events and Maintaining Historical Events in General

ACTions, A Book of Relational Insights

CHAPTER ONE

The Dark Pasture

In the waning light of the day, a gentle breeze danced across the grass of a pasture where thirty sheep had just been relocated. It would take some time for the animals to graze down the area and, with the new spring growth, each animal would be able to find a spot and contentedly munch to fill its four stomachs. Last year's lambs had grown through the winter and spring and, now that they were in an area much larger than a pen, were apt to chase each other; frolicking and jumping over one and another. They had a limitless store of energy and, as energetic youngsters, made a general nuisance of themselves around the other older sheep which would attempt to headbutt and kick at the yearlings. The young sheep, however, would merely spring into the air and make a game out of avoiding the older sheep.

In their playfulness, the young animals were oblivious to the danger lurking on the edge of the pasture, just inside a shelter belt and downwind from their noses. Numerous brown and black forms slunk through the brush inside the tree line and eventually crept out, into the pasture amid the small hillocks and bumps. They were wild dogs, six of them. Each one had slowly moved out, crouched down low to the ground and remained in place. In the short space of a minute all were lying on their bellies, with legs gathered underneath, ready to spring into action.

The leader of this pack of dogs was a large shepherd-cross that was the closest to the unwitting sheep. There was, in the countenance of this pack leader, no playfulness. His piercing copper eyes were fixed on his intended quarry. He was calculating distance, looking for the closest target, his ears were perked forward at full attention listening for any alarm or danger that would interfere with this next hunt.

The other five dogs were composed of a yellowish-red Irish setter female, two young male shepherds with brindling on their legs and neck, a black lab female with shepherd like ears and lastly a young male Airedale. All were poised to break into a run as soon as the leader made his move. Each of the others, with the exception of the black lab, had been socialized by the leader to follow his movements or pay the consequences of bloody bites and torn ears. They had seen several other "newcomers" be killed because of challenges to the leader's authority, his quick actions were merciless.

Now from underneath grey clouds scudding across the dim sky, came a venire of sunlight that touched the pasture and as the setting sun dipped below the horizon the leader sprang into action. His gate was quick and his attack decisive; striking the first lamb as it jumped into the air, he caught it by the back leg and with powerful jaws, sank his teeth into the muscle. His thick neck recoiled to bring the first victim down to the ground, spinning the legs away from his head and exposing the top of the lamb's back. A plaintive-bleat ushered from its mouth and in a second it was silenced by his jaws that clamped down on the throat like a vice, crunching bone.

In similar fashion each of the other dogs picked out a lamb, grabbed it by a hind leg to rip out the ham string. When the lamb was on its side, the throat was next and the animal was quickly suffocated. The two brindled males teamed up on a large ewe that kicked at them as she ran but when one bit at her flanks and tore the skin, she fell to the ground. The desperate ewe rolled over trying to rise up as her life's blood poured forth from her wounds. While one brindled male was at her throat the other tore at her belly exposing her organs. She tried to kick, but to no avail. Soon she lay lifeless.

The Dark Pasture

As each dog brought down a lamb for the kill, it quickly sought out another. The scene became a killing frenzy. The hunt became a slaughter having more to do with killing for the sake of killing rather than hunting to eat. In minutes all of the sheep were bunched up in a corner, pinned to the fence by other terrified comrades all of whom were bleating in the loudest manner. Several sheep being chased ran toward the protection of the herd and, in an effort to jump into the middle, actually launched over the fence and upon realizing their freedom continued to run. Seven in all were able to achieve escape in this fortuitous fashion and all came together and ran together no sheep in particular was really leading, but all were collectively following.

In the space of fifteen minutes twenty-three sheep lie dead and dying. Now there were no more bleats or sounds from the wooly herd, only the panting of the dogs as each one surveyed the pasture looking for something else to kill. Each dog then picked a carcass upon which to feed and ate until its belly was physically distended. The Airedale ate until he vomited and then after his convulsions had subsided, he returned to the carcass upon which he was feeding and began to gorge himself again. Soon all dogs were licking at their paws and legs attempting to clean the blood from their fur. Under the black of night, the pack finally slipped out of the pasture and back to their temporary home in a coulee leading to the Sheyenne River.

There had been many forays into the farmland in the last year. In each case, some sort of kill had been made. Whether it was one animal or several, goats, sheep, chickens, geese, ducks and on several occasions even large calves succumbed to the collection of fangs and bloodlust.

Their next big hunt for a calf was not going well. They attempted, a number of times, to approach a jumpy herd of cattle and single out a calf, but an impending early morning storm broke suddenly with severe lightning strikes, punctuated simultaneously by ear-splitting "pops" as if giant hands were slapping together over head. Peels of thunder began like the cracking of wood followed by a booming thunder. It seemed more like a war of immense cannons than it did a storm. The cattle began to bellow loudly as they divided into two groups each trying to avoid any contact from the wild dogs. The lightning grew more intense creating a disorienting affect. After the flash had dissipated, the eyes of cattle and dogs had to readjust and so there ensued for several seconds a blindness filled with the blue jagged shape of the most recent streak. A thick wave of hail fell hard for several minutes followed by the rain which came down in sheets dropping over an inch of water in a short amount of time. The combination of rain and hail pelted hard against the faces of both cattle and dogs, making it especially hard to keep the eyes open much less see. This most recent turn of events upset the pack's plan of making a kill. Twelve cattle; however, broke through the fence and began to head west-southwest, into the wind and away from the pursuing pack.

A short time later a red and gray Chevrolet pick-up drove down the driveway, past the cattle and with its appearance the pack made a hasty exit. The pick-up turned onto the county road and stopped at the mailbox. The pack leader kept his gaze fixed on the vehicle. When it stopped he turned and entered the nearby shelter belt; then turned again to sit and watch.

The pick-up, with engine running and exhaust wafting into the morning air, made the leader anxious. He had been educated on several occasions. He had learned what to expect when humans exited a running vehicle. The long objects in their hands would suddenly spit fire followed by a loud crack of sound. The effects he noticed were that his nearby companions would yelp, fall to the ground and remain there lifeless. He had taken the time on the first incident to smell the hot blood of one of his lifeless comrades. In an effort to help he had moved closer and as he did, he felt a hot sting on one of his ears, causing him to instantly roll, gain his feet and run to the nearest set of woods. From that day forward, he did not trust stopped vehicles, especially with engines running. Never-the-less he was last to leave the area. His hunger made him reluctant to move-on; however, his experience had taught him survival was better than a full belly.

*   *   *

Cantry, a tall, lanky, young man, noticed later in the evening, many hours after the early morning storm had passed, that the fence was in need of repair and so he applied himself to the task. As he made the last of the twists in the repairs, he counted the cattle according to the colored tags in their ears and realized twelve were missing. After returning to the house he made a few phone calls to the neighbors. It was then they realized that no one had seen the cattle, which, left but one option. Someone would have to go looking for them. He and his uncle had taken different trucks along the roads. His uncle headed up to State 46 to Leonard and south to a cross road. Cantry on the other hand drove toward the sawmill road and south to the same cross road. Each then travelled down various gravel roads both north and south, east and west until they both met at the intersection where the Sawmill road crossed the road to Walcott. Light was fading fast and further searching would be a waste of time. Neither having any luck, the only thing to do was to head out the next morning.

CHAPTER TWO

The Following Day

In the light of dawn, two figures, male and female, saddled up their horses, just outside the coral near the barn door. Each figure packed saddlebags and fitted them behind his and her respective saddles and then spent several minutes more checking straps, cinches and tie-downs. These last-minute checks were habit and usually nothing needed attention, but this morning the results yielded not only a problem but a new answer. In the process of packing a set of old saddle bags the young man tore the tongue from the flap on one bag. With nothing to feed the buckle, the bag was impossible to secure. On the other side of the set, the buckle itself tore from the body resulting again in a bag which could not be secured. He mumbled an epithet under his breath.

"What's the matter Cantry?" the young female asked.

"I dunno," came the answer. "I keep nursing these old bags along because Uncle Stan told me I could use them, but they are so old and dry-cracked that the leather is tearing."

"Well, maybe you could get some bailing twine and tie them shut." No reply followed. "What do you think?" she said as she plied him for an answer. Cantry still made no answer. She rounded the front of her horse and found him standing, staring at the back of his saddle. "Hey?" she prodded, looking for an answer.

"Yeah Jewel," he responded.

"What are you doing?" she asked in a mumbled voice. But before he could answer, another voice came from the yard.

"Cantry, if those bags are getting too old, why don't you take that 'wall-bag' or what-ever you call it and use it instead"

"Oh, hey Uncle Ian," the young man said with a start.

"Morning Mr. Thorvig," came the greeting from Jewel. "We didn't know you were up."

"Morning to you too Jewel. Yeah, it's hard to stay in bed when there's activity about. Say, you sure you're not going to get bored? There's no barrels out there to race around." Uncle Ian's sharp wit was always in play.

Jewel flashed a smile. As she shook her head at the comment, then responded, "As long as I'm in the saddle, I hardly ever get bored."

Cantry, quickly followed his uncle's suggestion with "What you said earlier, what do you mean?"

"I don't know." Uncle Ian said as he walked toward them. "What are you asking about; my inability to sleep, or Jewel finding a barrel to race around or the...?

"What bag?" Cantry blurted out.

Uncle Ian smiled, "You know, that odd bag, that double bag with the slit up the middle, that you got at that muzzleloader trade show a couple months ago. Why don't you use that thing. I'm sure my brother wouldn't mind if you pitched those old bags. They're pretty used-up."

Cantry held his gaze on his uncle's visage for a few seconds before he broke the silent pause. "Wallet...the trader called it a wallet." His eyes looked to the ground and began to dart around as he thought and soon his head was bobbing slightly.

"You said it could be tied on the back of the saddle, you know, like the pioneers would-a done. I'm sure Storm won't mind, the difference." Uncle Ian being a practical man, and not one to waste money, saw the bags, or rather wallet, as a viable alternative to replace the saddlebags.

Cantry's blank stare soon changed as his eyebrows raised up under the wide brim of his hat. He considered his uncle's suggestion. Then his eyes found their way back to his uncle. "Yeah, I guess I could," he pondered as he brushed at a fly buzzing around his head.

Continuing with his practical bent, Uncle Ian continued, "If you paid good money for 'em, they should be put to good use...ya-know?"

The item in question, a canvas wallet, was something Cantry had purchased at a recent black powder trade show in Fargo. It was a common form of bag, the style of which dated to the 1700's. It measured approximately forty-two inches long, sixteen inches wide sewn into a hollow tube, flat at the ends. It opened by means of a slit up the middle which created in effect a bag at either end. To close the item, the bag-ends were twisted in different directions which twisted the middle into a single collumn. It was simple, yet effective.

Cantry, headed into the house, fetched the wallet and came back out to the horses where he emptied the saddle bags and filled the wallet, making sure to balance the load. In the meanwhile, his uncle took up the saddle bags and brought them into the old barn. He pushed open the heavy wooden door. It made a rumbling noise, as the squeeky wheels from which it hung tracked along the hanger pipe. Instinctively he reached across with his left hand for the old brown bakelite covered wall switch which made a loud *click*. A shaft of bright light stretched into the pre-dawn dimness. Cantry, who could hear the door being opened quickened his pace from the house. As he approached, he moved into the light beaming from the open door of the barn, thankful for the opportunity to sort his items in the light.

Into the left side of his wallet Cantry placed his own five-band walky-talky radio. Though the radios were added bulk and weight, these could be used by Cantry and Jewel to communicate with each other if lost, as well as call back to the base-station at the house. It was a sign of the times. The Eighties were coming to a close and the Nineties were just around the corner. Farmers and ranchers everywhere were commonly using electronics to communicate, when out in the field. Some of the bigger outfits had even installed the new, and expensive, cellular phones in a few of their vehicles, which they found did not always work. There seemed to be large areas, called dead-zones, where no reception occurred. Because of that problem, many farmers continued to make use of the older CB radios, including Cantry's Uncle Ian.

Into the right side of his wallet Cantry placed a large tin cup with an additional smaller tin cup used as a cover to keep in the contents of sugar and baker's chocolate. He also brought some jerky, bread and two cans of cola. On his person Cantry tucked a sheath knife into the front of his belt and a small belt ax in the back of his belt. The handiness of both being strong suggestions from his uncle; again, since the young man had paid good money for them, he had better get some use out of them. At last, he tied the wallet just behind the cantle of the saddle and saw that it fit rather well and found some satisfaction in the new, but old-fashioned option.

Jewel, on the other hand, placed into her right saddlebag a two-band walky-talky radio and in her left bag, a set of flares and her new "pocket survival-tool" from Leatherman. She also outfitted herself with some bread, hotdogs, two cans of cola.

In addition to the food, each had a canteen of water, a lariat and that quintessential tool that no cattle owner went without... fencing pliers. Looking for twelve cattle, on the vast expanse of the prairie, or rather open grasslands, would be difficult especially when the animals had an eighteen-hour head start. However, the two were prepared to spend all day searching and, if push came to shove, remain overnight and thus each had a small bed-roll.

Ride in the Open Spaces

Finally, when both Cantry and Jewel were satisfied that their horses and gear were in order they mounted, and as they did a voice came from inside the barn. "Be careful, stay in touch."

"We will Uncle Ian," Cantry assured his uncle.

Reining their horses away from the barn, they rode into the small pasture, through the gate and into the larger field bordering the shelter belt. They came to a small trail, entered it and wound their way through the trees. Finally, they emerged out onto the open fields and headed south-southwest to the prairie-grasslands. The gradual brightening of the skies foretold the beginning of the day accompanied by the singing of birds. The grass, glistening with morning dew, was parted into two parallel tracks by the horses.

On the bay rode Jewel, a petite girl in her late teens, her blond hair bounced with the gate of the mare, who was called, Sandy, short for "Sandy Whirl-Wind." Though small, Jewel, had the confidence born of experience and her control of the bay was nothing less than total. On the appaloosa rode, Cantry, a lanky, wiry young man of nearly twenty. He and the horse maintained one rhythm as his posture in the saddle spoke of seasons spent straddling horse or pony, and who could have doubtless stayed upon the back of the animal while in a deep slumber.

Ahead lay a day of riding. Cantry was hoping to catch sight of the cattle before noon, but it might be longer if they could not pick up the trail. The weather had not turned hot quite yet and May was a mixed bag of temperatures and precipitation ranging from seventy-five degrees, in some years, to four inches of slushy-snow and cold winds in other years.

Some would treat this as work, but the two enjoyed riding and looked forward to it each week. A few of the rides could just as well have been dates. They were taken on Friday and Saturday afternoons and the two did not return, on some occasions until well after supper; much to the chagrin of both of her parents and his aunt and uncle.

The two were carefree and thoughts of school were far from their minds. Planting of the small grains would start in a week or so and it was not yet time for cutting hay, raking or baling. There had been a decent price for the flax straw from an itinerant linen buyer, who just happened to be making a round through the Dakotas. Since that straw had been baled up and hauled out last fall, that field would not have to be worked more than the others. There was nothing to do now except keep up with minor maintenance around the barnyard and get ready for summer. The cattle could not have slipped out at a better time.

The two stopped on a knoll near an east-west county road. Cantry lifted his thumb up to tip his hat back, squinted his eyes a bit, then related, "Ya' know Uncle Ian seems to' think that they headed for the river and will follow it down to the grasslands.

"Why does he think that?' queried Jewel.

"Well…I guess probably because they've headed that way before," he opined.

"Well I don't recall em going that way before, ya know," she answered smartly.

"Do you keep a close eye on 'em?" he asked.

"Hey now, what difference does that make?" she said a little irritated.

"He probably knows them cows a heck of a lot better than you do… ya' know…so I'm gonna' go by what he said," he calmly retorted.

Jewel could tell he was just about to continue when she quipped, "Okay, okay, okay…I just never heard him talk about it. That's all I'm sayin' okay."

A short pause intervened between the two of them. The

silence was broken when one of the horses snorted. The other threw its chin forward to gain some slack in the reins and shook its head. The sound of the metal on the bridal clinking distracted Jewel who grabbed at the reins before the horse could stretch out its neck again.

Cantry added a stabbing remark, "Well, you asked!" his eyebrows lifted haughtily.

"OKAY!" Came another quick quip from Jewel who added her own one-ups-manship, "But I've looked for cows too ya' know."

"Well I ain't arguing with ya' there," he said rather meekly, knowing that he should not have zinged her with that last remark. She exhaled abruptly, shook her head and looked at him with a mocking gesture. Jewel was not one to stay angry or hold a grudge…usually.

Cantry responded to her gesture, "Whaa-aaat?" his tone falling as he vocalized the word.

"Nothing." she said defiantly. The bay was becoming restless. It thrust its chin outward again in an attempt to grab a mouth of some delectable new green grass. She reined her horse around to face him, doing her best to sport a serious countenance. She guided the bay up beside the appaloosa, stopped and gave him a peck on the lips. Then in a playful gesture she stole the hat from off of his head, tucked it into her belly then, with a mild barrel racing maneuver, turned and spurred her horse and galloped away.

"Hey. C'mon now. Give that ba'ock," his Minnesota enunciation being clearly discernable. He spurred his horse after Jewel. She slowed down as soon as he approached on his "steed" as he was apt to refer to his gelding. He quickly said in his own haughty way.

"You'd better watch out for gopher holes."

"Uh huh," she responded, "I learned to ride around here too…remember?"

"Yeah, I s'pose," he said agreeably.

She returned his hat, but continued in her attempt to bait him, "Besides, I not trying ta' rope anything…right?"

Cantry fumbled with his words and hat, "No. Uh, yeah right."

She continued, "Anyways, I automatically look for bad ground whenever I ride."

Cantry smirked, shook his head and deliberately closed his mouth with a thump, signaling that he was not going to dig himself any deeper into this banter, even though it was more playful than serious. There was no discussion for a while. Whether it was barrel racing, roping, or as in this instance, conversation, one thing was for sure, Jewel could hold her own.

The two followed the trail through the occasional muddy patch where the rain had not washed tracks away completely. The sign was now leading them straight west.

Sometime later, breaking the silence, Jewel asked, "Did those guys ever figure anything out for a barbeque or pig roast or what ever?"

'I dunno," replied Cantry. He continued, "You mean Curty and Sinster?"

"Mm, hmm," she said with a nod.

"I wouldn't mind a big picnic, hey. It's been a while for me 'cause I missed the celebrations on the Fourth, last year chasin' after them stupid wild dogs. Actually, we all missed the big feed."

"You going to be ready for them now with that antique?"

"You mean the Henry?" At that moment he reached back with his right hand to remove the lever action rifle from its scabbard. Its brass receiver still appeared new in contrast with the dark blued barrel and tubular magazine. The wood on the butt stock was finished with many coats of linseed oil giving it a deep red-brown finish.

She nodded her head quickly as she watched him rest the rifle with the butt stock on his thigh.

"Yeah, I'll be ready. I just loaded up some 44-40 shells the other day. Matter of fact it's loaded right now. See, this little knob is pushed up towards this slot here where the bullets go in. That shows it's full… and it's not an antique," he corrected her. "It's a reproduction rifle just like they made 'em back in the 1800's." His words lingered in the air for a bit. "By the way, I'm real glad that you talked me in ta' going to that black powder cartridge shoot last year. This Henry actually shoots just as good if not better than my forty-four semi-auto. Thanks."

Jewel quietly said, "You're welcome." Her faced beamed from the appreciation.

Without more he slipped the rifle back into its scabbard and changed the subject back to food, a subject ever-present on a young man's mind or rather stomach. "Half a beef roasted over hardwood." He said as he looked up, rolling it over in his mind. "Yeaaaaah" he said almost imperceptibly as the wheels in his mind were turning over and over at the thought of a picnic. "Corn on the cob…with lots of butter and… ice cold root beer," he continued as he thought out loud. A grin slowly crept onto his face as he came out of his trance. He took in a deep breath, exhaled and began to look at the ground followed by darting glances at the horizon.

Jewel kept her gaze on Cantry for some time before he turned his head in a "double-take" motion.

"What?"

"I dunno. I'm kind'a curious about the whole…" she paused for a moment as she mentally drafted her question, then began by phonetically pronouncing the word, "Ron-Dee-Voo camping with old-timey guns and clothes thing. Why is it so…" she paused again.

"Why is it so interesting to you? I mean, there's lots of hobbies like race cars, dirt bikes, remote controlled airplanes, video games like Pac-Man, Super-Mario Brothers and stuff like that. Why all the old-fashioned stuff?"

Cantry smiled, took a breath and began, "Ok, for a lotta folks it starts with a muzzleloader, usually a rifle. First, it has to be loaded with powder from a horn, then a lead ball in a patch of cloth, then the ram-rod to push the patched ball down the barrel and the one shot. So, the guys who shoot 'em, and women too; ya know, they only get one shot so they have to make it count. It's fun to shoot at paper targets or try to hit little objects like pieces of charcoal, or completely clip the vane of a feather, or hit two small sticks where they cross."

"Yeah, I get all that," Jewel interrupted him suddenly, "but why do you or anyone get dressed in funny clothes and camp out? And, by the way, you don't have a muzzle loader yourself, instead you have a rifle that has shells. I think you called it a "cartridge gun.""

"CA'ridge gun," said Cantry as he tried to mimic a New England accent. "The word is pronounced Ca' ridge." He could tell he had confused her by the "deer in the headlight look." Then he added, "It's an inside joke among those of us who shoot muzzleloaders; and yes, I do have a muzzleloader that I use, it's Uncle Ian's rifle. It is a Thompson/Center-Hawken, Fifty caliber, cap-lock rifle. I was shooting that before I bought the Henry. Uncle Ian helped me when I was trying to decide to purchase a gun, um, he said he would continue to let me use his T C Hawken if I bought the Henry. So, long before I bought the Henry, I started by shooting his muzzleloader. We went to some camps where all they shot were the older muzzleloaders. This was before anyone had any competitions with the cartridge guns. And…" he turned to look at Jewel whose brows were knitted, trying to follow his explanation. He continued, "I'm not answering the question, am I?

"Huh-uh," she replied shaking her head her mouth slightly open and her gaze fixed on Cantry, as if waiting for some epiphany. It was clear that she was trying to understand, but like a match to damp tinder, nothing was catching. "Why can't you just wear regular clothes and stay in a modern tent?"

"Oh yeah, clothing..." Cantry returned, then continued, "when people start to use the guns, from that time, they also begin to ask themselves, what was available in the pre 1840's? What did they actually wear? What all did they make with their hands?' I also had to ask myself, besides hunting and shooting, how do I cook on a fire, like they did?' What did they live in? I sure didn't know, but I wanted to learn."

He took a breath and began to answer his questions, "That's why some who are really serious about history, won't have any plastic, nylon or aluminum. They'll only use glass, wood or tin for containers. They figure that if Daniel Boone didn't have it in 1775, then neither should they. That's why some of the participants, wear clothes that are identical to the hunters in 1770, or soldiers in the Revolutionary War of 1775 to 1783. The clothes from then, are only made from linen, wool, cotton, even hemp, like the fabrics that existed two hundred and twenty years ago, That's why ya' see people getting knives and axes made by a blacksmiths instead of the hunting store. And instead of getting their cookware from the fleet store they get their tin cups and brass cooking kettles from a tin-smith. There are wood-workers who fit boxes together with dove-tailed joints and use real wood; not plywood. Heck, they even had a broom maker the one year, who used real "broom-corn" to make his brooms that date to 1825, I think."

He peered down at the ground for a moment, then raised

his head to look at Jewel, "This is not fantasy. It's real black powder, knives, axes, tents, leather, and camp-fires all aimed at trying to live-out a lifestyle. People actually lived by hunting, trapping, fishing, riding horses, here in Dakota since the late 1700's. This land used to be wild, untamed. So for me havin' a muzzleloader, just feels right. The clothes are real too and based on clothing that folks wore back then. That's why I hate it when people call them costumes. Ok, so, does that answer your question?" He was fairly certain he had fully fleshed out the points he had identified. He looked at Jewel, who, was giving him a sideways glance.

"You were saying about cooking fires?" she prompted.

Cantry thought. "Oh yeah...a bit of a mixed-bag there, as I understand it. We see a lotta cast iron at the camp fire but I'm told that most of that stuff, I mean cast iron, stayed home where it was used at the hearth. It's just so stinkin' heavy to lug that around on a horse. I s'pose if a family were moving to a new place it would be in the wagon, so maybe in that case it could be at the camp fire. The hunters and Indians and explorers would take with them lightweight stuff like tinned steel, or tinned lined copper and brass, a small sheet-iron fry-pan. But anyway, the whole idea is to use only the stuff that the hunters, or pioneers, or settlers actually used at that time."

He paused again to collect his thoughts, "Um… it takes research and reading to see what they actually had available to them, which is where the term 'period' is used to describe stuff. So, like, period shoes would be buckle shoes in the 1700's, or moccasins same thing. Ya' don't see rubber boots, or at least yer not supposed to see 'em, because they did not exist and people just used leather boots or shoes or moccasins. Period hats, period guns, period cookware, period tents, means those things are based-on that period in time."

"So, it's a competition?" Jewel inquired.

"The short answer is no. You would only be competing against yourself. What are you willing to settle for, in terms of stuff that's correct for that time and that region? If the camper cares about getting it right, then the stuff in camp can be documented versus a camp that looks like a flea market. As far as any other competition, well, I guess if your selling stuff, and trying to get people to buy your stuff instead of someone else's, then maybe it is a competition. But it goes deeper…it's…" Cantry again found himself searching for further explanation.

He continued, "I think you'll find that a lotta folks are eager to share their research or discuss the books that they have read. In the movie we watched on TV last weekend, *The Northwest Passage,* Spencer Tracy plays the part of the New England, frontiersman and explorer, Robert Rogers. He was a real person. Rogers, like a lot of people of the time, kept a journal. His descriptions give the reader a glimpse into the everyday life at that time. Some of us are searching for that historical feeling when we watch the movie. I did learn a short time ago that the clothing used in the movie is not correct for the time period.

"I guess what happened is, a Hollywood art director de-signed some goofy romantic junk that… I dunno, looked like Robin Hood only Six Hundred years too late. The setting of the movie is supposed to be based on the French and Indian War from about 1755 or 56 up to 1763. The clothing should be colonial. It's a no-brainer. That's when the story takes place. The clothing should reflect that time and place; not some artsy-fartsy modern interpre-tation. Well, anyway, after I saw the movie the first time, I found and read a book about him based on his journal. In the journal, he wrote about how to fight and how to move through the woods. That's the cool part. A guy named, Kenneth Roberts, authored book and it has the same name as the movie."

He quickly looked at Jewel and continued, "ok, I'm getting off track a little bit. It's…it's fun to get it right. It feels like I've accomplished something good when I can base my gun, shirt, hat, boots, knife or tent on a time period. Maybe it's based on a person that is mentioned in a journal written back in that time. If I can accurately recreate that, it's like I'm living in a part of history; like I've just stepped out of history itself. Does that make sense?"

Jewel, who began to nod her head, looked at Cantry, and abruptly changed her gesture, to shaking her head "No." Her brow remained knitted as she thought about his words. "But why does it matter if you have the right style of shirt?

Cantry's response came rather quickly, "Because…it matters because, back then that's what they wore and today so can I. You learn what that style of clothing feels like, you find out what works and what doesn't. I don't need or want the modern camping stuff. Besides, I defy you to go to a department store or hardware store to find any of the stuff you see at camp. With the exception of a few of the sporting goods stores that have round balls and caps for shooting and kits to make your own muzzleloader, it can't be found. The stores don't keep up with that old stuff; all they want to do is sell the latest fashion or some 'wiz-bang' gun scope and water-proof boots." He looked back at her and she was still shaking her head.

"Wouldn't it just be easier to buy stuff at the store, or use modern camping stuff? You can always just read about it. Cant ya?"

"No, that's not it. It's not about being easier. It's about the experience of what it was like two hundrd years ago. I want to use *only* the clothing and camp items that they had back then."

Jewel was still shaking her head.

He thought about her love of the Ford Mustang cars and with that idea in mind he began again. "Ok, you wouldn't see someone putting a 1972 Dodge Dart hood on a 1967 Ford Mustang, would you?

"Heck no!" Her response came quickly, "That'd be pretty stupid. They don't go together. If I ever get a Mustang, it's not gonna have anything on it except stuff for a Ford."

"Exactly!" Cantry responded. "You also wouldn't see someone trying to put a hood from a modern Ford pick-up on a Model-T either. Historically, it's out of place. All the fringe that you see in the romantic Hollywood films, for instance, and all the dangly-stuff hanging down from the big furry coyote hats, are not historically correct. That fancy stuff was mostly used for a stage-play, a show or a fair. The only way to see if it works is to use it and learn. Besides, that stuff just gets in the way when it is used in real life. It gets caught on brush or tangled in other equipment."

"By using the clothes with the rifle and pouch and powder horn it should all work together like a well-designed system. It's more than clothing though. It's what some call a "kit" meaning all the stuff used at camp, including food, tools, blankets, shipping boxes and the lack of other stuff. It really is fun to get things right, not just historical clothing but everything. Some folks say, 'don't do your research by watching Hollywood movies.' That bein' said, ya have to crack a book; and don't just read, but study what's written."

"OK," her voice emanated in the tone of a question, "but you still haven't explained that you are shooting a gun from the mid 1860's, but the other stuff you have is before 1840."

"That's a good point. I have the Henry because it's a cool rifle and I've always wanted a lever action, but I won't be using that at a pre-1840's camp. That aside, there's a rule of thumb that is easy to apply. That rule is: it's ok to have something in camp from some-years before a date, but it can't be after, because that item did not exist yet. For example; if I wanted to portray someone in history who would have used the Henry, then my clothes and other stuff should match this 1860's gun, I could have a felt hat from 1860, or before, same with the shirt, and riding boots from that time as well. Maybe I'd have a McClelland sort of saddle, which by the way are made for really bony horses, but that's another matter. I'd also have a pistol up next to my belt buckle; what they call a 'cross draw' holster, not the ones that are low slung half-way down the thigh like Hollywood actors. Those low holsters are just askin' for a pistol to fall out when you're on horseback, and get lost."

He took a deep breath and continued, "so, if I wanted to use the kind of clothes that were worn in 1860 or 1865 then my clothes would be correct for the time of my rifle. Actually, I do have that heavy wool coat that looks like a civil war coat but without any decoration. I didn't bring it because I thought it would be way-too-hot. Maybe I shoulda' brought it and taken the chance to learn by using it while I'm working. I just figured we' d find the cows by now."

He thought about a slightly different approach. "Ok, think about the guys that you saw at the cartridge shoot, …where I bought the Henry. Think back, what they looked like. I believe they were trying to portray pre 1870's. Even still, those guys are also involved in shooting competitions out in Wyoming and Montana. They are a good example of folks who do stuff in the West, in a later time period. They use lever actions and revolvers together, as well as double barrel shot-guns, not to mention guns like the .45-70 Sharps and other guns used to hunt buffalo. Their clothing matches the time period and place but its more than just clothes. Those camps also should have the sorts of equipment and cookware and tents that existed in 1867 or 1870, that is, if they care about getting it all correct to the period. I guess you could say that the people who do this don't want things that are out-of-place for that time. The extreme example would be a 1967 Mustang car at a jousting match in England in the year 1215. Obviously it doesn't fit. It's way out of place. That's why there's limits on the years. A lot of camps are pre 1840, but some are a short span like 1812 to 1815. There's others that are strictly Civil War in the years 1861 to 1865. It would be a whole lotta work to set up a camp, just to get it wrong. I, myself, don't want something out of place; if I can help it. It would ruin the ah... ambience...for me. Actually, it would be kind of unfair to my neighbors at camp, 'cause it would basically ruin their experience too." Cantry noticed that Jewel's expression had changed.

The squinting eyes and the knitted eyebrows had been replaced in Jewel's countenance as if she had been brightened by an internal lamp. She was noticeably taken with a wave of new thought. "It sounds as if the rendezvous gives you a place to use your stuff for several days, not just guns, but anything in camp...everything in camp it seems? So, it all gets used, or tested, at the same time, and it should all fit together in that part of history. Hmm, I guess you're testing yourself too... with your equipment, and your knowledge of history, aren't you? I guess it's really more than...it's a whole lot more than just a bunch of dates. Isn't it?"

Cantry turned to look her in nodding approval and with a smile simply said, "Yep! It's a work in progress. The best part of period camps, whether your totally correct or not, is the feeling of being blended into the experience; or I guess maybe *woven* into it would be a better way to say it. Attending camps with others who enjoy them, is part of the camaraderie. I like to learn. I also like to share and to keep on honing my historical ways. That's the part that gives me satisfaction. I s'pose others would agree with that. Ya know?"

CHAPTER THREE

From Empty Coulees to Open Spaces

Jewel and Cantry rode in silence for some time searching for the herd. Occasionally one of them would peel off of their general route to investigate a likely ravine or island of trees or clump of scrub where the cattle had been but had since vacated the scene. There were no words, just a tacit understanding of their basic duties. Other sign, such as hoof prints and cow pies, though washed out, were evidence of their passage. So far, there was very little sign, which meant that the cattle were moving awfully fast; as if being pursued. The thought entered Cantry's mind that predators might be a problem and he reached down to make sure his Henry rifle was secure in its scabbard. "I hope it's not dogs." he munbled to himself.

He had no sooner mouthed the words when he saw in the distance several crows circling about and landing in a dead elm near the river. "Oh no." he whispered to himself. He merely pointed at the crows. His gesture caught Jewel's attention and then he reined his mount in that direction. Jewel did likewise. It was not far off, but Cantry wanted to be prepared. After shifting the reins to his left hand, he leaned over and removed the Henry from its scabbard and laid it just behind the pommel of the saddle. He kept the reins in his left hand, held over-top-of the Henry. Though the rifle remained un-cocked, it was now "in-hand;" ready for quick use. When Jewel saw that the muzzle of the rifle was pointed to his left she stopped the bay to let him pass, then turned to ride up along his right side.

Soon the cawing sound of the crows became prominent as more of them lifted off of the trees near the coulee. They flew back and forth in a tight area which foretold of something dead and therefore a meal. With that many birds, it must be a fairly large animal.

As the two riders approached the area, the terrain fell away toward the river. Finally, they were able to peer into the ravine, where they spotted the unmistakable sign of blood. The scene they had come upon revealed a fight where calf had been killed and afterwards, pulled apart. The entrails were strung out, away from the carcass and the front shoulder and back ham had been eaten away down to the bone. At that Cantry dismounted, switched the rifle to his left hand, pulled the reins over Storm's head. Without taking his eyes off of the ravine he walked around the front of Storm and with his right, handed the reins to Jewel who stayed in the saddle. He cocked the rifle. The wind was dead calm in this sheltered area.

As Cantry approached the carcass, he looked for a tag but was pretty sure that he was looking at one of his uncle's cattle. He quietly squatted down under an ash tree and surveyed the coulee for any movement. The last thing he wanted to do was to startle anything like wild dogs. He had a feeling that this was their doing. If they were still in the area, he did not want to get too close, too soon and force a hand-to-fang fight with them. His cautious nature overrode his curiosity and he stayed under the shade of the box-elder tree to observe.

When he was satisfied that nothing like a dog or coyote was guarding the bloody mess he approached in a circular fashion so as not to disturb any sign that might be a clue and then he saw in the grass, an ear tag that had obviously been ripped out of the ear when the calf was being brought down for the kill. Mid-stride, he stopped to listen for what sounded like the rustling of brush. As he turned his head slowly, he was searching for a familiar shape whether it was, a fox, or 'coon; something that would be naturally drawn up from the river to the kill site.

Off to his left he saw a twig on a brush pile that was bouncing when it should have been still. He turned toward the moving twig, thumbed back the hammer and raised the rifle. Within several steps he began to hear growling and he tried to discern the shape of a dog or coyote. With the rifle to his shoulder, he focussed on the growl. His eyes were trained on the sound in or near the brush pile. He strained to see anything, but as he reconoitered the edge, he was now convinced that what ever it was, had crawled into the pile for protection. He continued to circle to his left, slowly advancing clockwise around the brush pile.

After many small steps, he could finally see a wrinkled snout and bared teeth. The growling became snarling which became more intense, so much so that it sounded like choking as the agitated beast inhaled. It barked within the growl, quickly followed by a yelp. Soon, there was heavy, labored breathing; the sort that belies extreme pain. The animal's breathing slowed, the low growling began and in seconds it lead to snarling again.

Cantry thought to himself that this is one of the dogs in the pack and obviously it is hurt, no doubt the calf had kicked or stepped on it in the fight. He continued to circle around until he could get a clear opening on the head, then he raised the rifle until the sights lined up on the ear and neck. If it was a rabid dog, he did not want to spray the brains into the air so he avoided the shot between the eyes.

His heart was beating heavily in his ears and he could feel his breathing change. As the dog took a breath for another round of growling, he squeezed the trigger and lost sight of the animal in a puff of white smoke. The next several seconds moved in slow motion as he levered down. The spent shell came flipping out of the top of the receiver; as it did he could hear the audible "ching" of the empty brass and the new shell "thunk" from the tubular magazine into the receiver. He pulled on the lever, and could hear the lift-arm within the receiver raise the shell. As the lever was brought to rest against the wrist stock, the shell was pushed into the chamber ready to shoot again. The butt stock never left his cheek and his eyes remained on the barrel and sights. He stood for several seconds waiting for any movement as time assumed a normal pace again.

He could hear the cawing of crows as they flew away…but there was no more growling. He kept the gun up and ready to fire again. He took a deep breath amid a rapid heart beat and then let it out slowly. Finally he said audibly, "there, one of yours for one of ours."

He brought the cocked hammer from full to a rest on half-cock as he still had a shell in the chamber. He reached into his vest pocket where he had four or five shells and replaced the cartridge he had just burnt. He moved forward a dozen steps to grab a branch on the ground. Using the branch, he pushed at the lifeless form, then reaching down took hold of the front paw to drag the dog from the brush pile. He could see that the back legs were curled to one side and figured it had sustained a busted hip or backbone. Either way, it was dead and now it was time to find the herd, hopefully eleven of them. He headed up out of the coulee to Jewel who still held the horses.

"Oh, my goodness I could almost see everything. Is there anything we need to do before we leave? she said excitedly.

"Naw, let's keep looking. The Score is one to one." Cantry adamantly stated as he mounted. "How'd the horses do?"

"Other than flinching some at the shot, they didn't spook at the blood and guts. Maybe they can't smell it here at the top of the ravine." Jewel reflected on the "score card" statement. Though she loved her dogs she was not sad at seeing the snarling dog get shot, she felt confident with Cantry's actions. She handed off the reins and was ready to get on the trail again.

The two headed to the next low area as they followed some sign to the west. Jewel kept to the high ground with its own share of ditches and Cantry down in the coulees that headed to the river. As each likely ravine or coulee turned out to be empty the investigating rider would make eye contact with the other and with a shake of the head come riding back. They resumed their general direction but now moved away from the river. Soon they angled onto the gravel road and followed it for nearly two miles before coming to a north-south road where they halted their search. They discussed the option of each taking a direction and if the cattle were found then to radio the other, so Cantry headed north towards the river. Jewel headed south where there were a few pockets that usually held water. She had gone nearly three quarters of a mile when she spotted cow pies and fresh tracks whereupon she quickly radioed Cantry who arrived in about fifteen minutes.

"What do you think?" Jewel asked.

"What are they doing this far south?" Cantry queried.

"So you think it's them?"

"Oh yeah. I don't see any other cattle herds roaming the area. Probably a good thing they crossed here 'cause this stretch looks like CRP.[1] Maybe all the way to the Grasslands.[2] But what in the heck are they doing this far south …and west?"

"It seems kinda' like the dogs are staying away from the roads and maybe the cattle are trying to stay on the roads? What do ya' think?"

Cantry did not answer right away but pondered Jewel's observation. He looked at the horizon and then to Jewel and said, "Could be!"

"OK, so…" began Jewel with a pause, "what happened last year when you went after those dogs?"

"Huh!" he began, his exasperation evident as he recalled the overall ordeal, "I got a call from, Curty, uh, actually Uncle Ian took the call, found me in the barn and handed me the phone. Curty, said he was heading up our way to take a look at a few areas where some neighbors had seen about seven dogs all running together. There were two huge blackish brown shepherd dogs that had come into some farm yards and had been so bold that they chased a woman and kids into the house. At another farm yard they tried to get at someone, I think one of the Jermsteads, or maybe Ericksons in the garage. So, anyway, we drove in two vehicles and I guess Curty spotted the dogs trotting across a field so he had the driver, stop on the other side of a shelter belt to intercept them in an ambush when they emerged by a shallow ditch. Okay, here's where it got really dicey."

Cantry paused for several seconds and then began, "Curty got out of the truck, with the loaded rifle and by the time he checked his shell in the chamber one of the two big shepherd dogs was already out of the shelter-belt and running, STRAIGHT AT HIM! He had just enough time to put the sights on him and pull the trigger. Well… he dropped the dog which tumbled to a stop about eight or ten feet from where he stood. He chambered another round and waited for it to move but it did not. So he started to look for the other to shoot as well, but it never appeared. I drove up a couple of minutes later and he had put on a pair of gloves to pull the dog into the shelter belt. He left it for the worms. I think that shook him a little and it's really hard to shake him."

"Then, we circled the area for a couple of hours trying to spot more of those dogs, especially that other shepherd. That continued until almost dark. I think it was about 9:30 or later when we finally called it quits. We thought we had 'em in those two quarter sections. We kept on looking with binoculars to spot them again but they holed-up or just disappeared in the terrain and low spots where we weren't looking." Cantry looked down and shook his head, then looked over to Jewel and shrugged his shoulders, as if to say, "*What can you do?*"

Though they had been out for several hours there was still dew in the shadow of a small knoll and all at once Cantry threw out his right hand with a rapid, "Hold it! Hold it! Stop."

Jewel snapped her head to the left to look at him. She could see he was looking ahead. As she glanced back at him, he began to speak.

"Look down in the dew. Ya' see them tracks?" he pointed as he leaned out away from his saddle. Both riders withdrew and then circled around a bit to get a better angle on the sunlight against the fading dew and thereby see the line of travel in the paths through the grass.

"Hmm. There's a bunch of tracks. Hope it's them," she said not taking her eyes off of the tracks.

"Well," Cantry said, "there's only one way to find out." He reined his horse to the left of the tracks and Jewel did likewise. For the next fifteen minutes or so they followed the trail at a fast walk. However, as a result of the sun and rising breezes, the dew quickly disappeared and with it, the trail. They still had the general direction of the cattle and therefore continued but the trail was turning west-southwest again.

Cantry was puzzled. The river was north of here but the cows were headed almost due west. "Does the river curve to the north and east at the edge of the grasslands? Or is there another small creek or water source due west of here?" he asked Jewel without looking at her, while his eyes scanned the horizon.

Jewel shrugged her shoulders, "I dunno." She murmured. "I think there are some small water holes between here and the river but I can't say exactly where they are."

He turned his head to look at her "Well when you were younger did you ever come this way or ride through here," he nodded his head in the direction of their travel. "I mean you were raised not too far from here. Right?"

"Ah, yeah I was and yeah, I think so...the river goes... It's just." Jewel stood up in her saddle to sweep the horizon, then sat down. "Well we've done a lotta ridin' on the trails in the grasslands, but I've never came at 'em from this way. I don't even know who owns this land..."

"What? What is it?" Cantry watched her as she reined Sandy to the left, the right and then left again.

"I'm just getting my bearings." She continued, "I think the river does...um," she continued to look and consider her position and the local geography. "I think it flows through the north part. It kinda' meanders up and down, I mean north and south, and then it cuts to the east, but by that time its heading almost straight north-east towards Kindred where the river cuts just north of the sawmill. So from where we are, and to the west, hmm... I think it's about three miles to the northwest from where we crossed County Road 18. But before we get there we'd cross, Oh gosh... I think it's... Highway 23? Then, there's a whole lotta' nothin' unless we hit a rid-ing trail; and that's way south of the horse camp." She paused again still scanning the horizon.

"Oh, okay. I..."

"Why." She inquired as she interrupted him.

"...hope we find them before they get that far. I mean its like they are heading for Sheldon."

Jewel turned to look at him with a look that spoke of unbe-lief. "Sheldon! Naaman, I hope we find them before they get even half that far."

"Well we're probably half that far already," Cantry said with a deflated tone to his voice.

She continued to stare at him while he removed his hat and brushed his forehead with his shirt sleeve. "Nice mohawk, hey," she said teasingly.

"There ain't no mohawk on my head, my hair's too short." He quickly retorted and a little unsure of himself. Of course, he did not have a mohawk but he did have a good case of "hat-hair." He brushed his hair this way and that and as he was doing so Jewel rode up to him fighting a grin on her lips. She grasped his hat first with one hand and then the other and studied it as though it were a stick ready to break over her knee. "Here, let me put that back on," she offered.

All he could do was to sit there and with a wince he uttered "Really? You really have to do this?"

"Oh yeah," she returned, "or else I'll keep it."

He sat there as she stood up in the stirrups, held the broad brimmed Resistol over his head and then gingerly placed it back on his head, making sure it was just right. Cantry remained there slumped waiting for some trick. It looked as if Jewel was about to sit down when she suddenly crammed the hat down over his forehead, pushing the tops of his ears out in the process causing Jewel to snicker. Rather than fight it he just sat there. He extended his lower lip and eventually pushed up the brim of his hat with his thumb while mimicking a "dumb" expression, then said in a rather dull voice, "Howdy there Ma'am." It was his impersonation of the stereotypical cowboy character from the old western shows, which Jewel referred to as "dusty old westerns." The mutual antics led both of them to giggling uncontrollably for some time. Finally, Jewel expelled a tired sigh; a hint which Cantry immediately understood.

As if on que, both dismounted, led the horses over to a

clump of trees next to a feeder stream to take a break. Cantry untied his wallet enough to retrieve some bread and jerky then pulled his Henry rifle from the scabbard and brought it with him to sit down. A nice breeze was blowing in their faces now, the horses grazed just down-wind behind them, where Jewel had tied off the mare. The gelding, though not tied, stayed by the mare. Jewel grabbed several of the colas and placed them into the cool feeder stream, still swollen from the rain, before she joined Cantry in the shade.

While the two of them unwrapped the bread and jerky, Jewel slowly moved a quizzical eye towards the rifle which Cantry had leaning against his shoulder, she could tell he was in deep thought.

"You'd think those cows would be happy just to sit in one place and graze and not roam all over the countryside." Cantry said.

Jewel, still looking at the shiny brass receiver on the rifle, then perked up, "Yea, I think this is kinda far. It would be a puzzle if we hadn't come across the dead calf and the dog. Still, we shoulda' spotted them cows by now, shouldn't we?" She turned her head to scan the open grassland, her head slowly rotated back and forth. "I think we must have missed that first road coming down from the north. We should'a hit it by now.

"Yeah...yeah," he said, half listening, still collecting his thoughts.

Jewel got up and quickly fetched the two cans of cola which were now much cooler and no doubt less volatile. She wiped the water from both of them, opened hers and, upon handing one to Cantry, he opened his. Each took a long drink, gulp after gulp before lowering the can, followed by an "air wash;" that contented sound of feeling refreshed. Jewel looked over at Cantry and began to wince, waiting for...

"BELLLLLCH!" came the sound from the young lad's throat

to which Jewel replied.

"Yep, and there it is; the All-Male chorus of soda-pop," she said as she shook her head and body.

Cantry fairly inhaled his piece of bread while Jewel continued to nibble on hers. The jerky took more time to chew and for some time the two sat there chewing without any conversation. Jewel kept turning her gaze to the rifle.

"So…what is the rifle for?"

Cantry took a breath and replied, "Okay, as long as we're sittin' here I figured that I might want to have it in my hands just in case I see something. Sorta' like sittin' in the deer stand and nothing moves for the first twenty or thirty minutes and then, the woods go about their business and animals start to move. If I see a coyote or some wild dogs, I want it right here, where I can reach it in a heartbeat."

"Is it ready to shoot?"

"Oh yah," he said as he gave her a glance. "I don't have anything chambered, but all I have to do is to lever a shell in like I did earlier, and it will be ready to fire. Ready to go. Ready to knock 'em down!" His redundant remarks were a bold reminder that he was a good shot and would not hesitate to use the rifle again to kill a coyote or wild dog.

After a few silent minutes, Jewel yawned, "You care if I take a nap," Jewel asked faintly as her jaw recovered from the reflex. Her eyes were closed as she lifted her head to catch the gentle breeze. The sugar in the soda and food were catching up to her and all she wanted to do was grab a few winks.

"Nope, you go ahead. I'm gonna' sit here and watch. Maybe someone or somethin' will come following that field road. It's probably too soft to drive on though."

Jewel made no remark. Indeed, a brief nap was next on the

agenda of what had turned out to be quite a long morning; at least seven hours in the saddle. Their search was now rolling into noon without any sight of the cattle. Within an hour though, both riders were back in the saddle and hot on the trail. Their search had brought them up to a cross road and the cattle were still heading west but had turned to the southwest. The riders had encountered some fenced off areas of grassland that were no doubt from a farm; the grain bins of which were poking up above the trees. As they rode further through some trees, they encountered a trail.

"Hey!" Jewel exclaimed, "I think I know this trail. It's the one that comes from that campground that's up the road; the one we just crossed.

"This is ridiculous! How far can those cows go in thirty-some hours. They've crossed a bunch of open la..." Cantry's words trailed off as he thought in silence. His eyes darted around as he thought. He halted and sat in the saddle with an emphatic breath began ranting to himself, " Ahhh! Stupid, blind idiot!"

Jewel reined her horse around to face him with a dubious gesture she asked, "What is it? What's the matter? Who's stupid...a blind idiot?"

Cantry cast his gaze into the sky, "we just spent a lotta time looking in the coulees and when we did find something it was a kill site. The cattle are trying to stay IN THE OPEN! Duh!" He looked at Jewel shaking his head as he continued to berate himself. "If they go into the coulees it is too tight of a place and that's why they keep moving because it is harder to sneak up on them. They can't get cornered. They're in the open." He then repeated with more emphasis, "They are going to stay in the open! They'll at least want to be in a whole-lot more open place than a coulee with high banks."

The wind had shifted and was out of the northwest, so any sounds ahead of them could not be heard until close upon the source. After fifteen minutes or so of riding, Cantry noticed the gelding's ears perk up. He then caught a sound of something himself. It was a bawling like that made by a calf. He was not sure of the direction so he watched the swiveling ears of his mount again. Finally, the gelding fixed his ears and head in a direction and held them there while he stared. The area was well treed with large cotton woods but fairly open underneath.

"What is it boy?" Cantry softly asked Storm as he stared in the same direction as the gelding. Then he turned in his saddle to face Jewel, "You hear that?" He whispered.

"Uh huh." she softly replied as she turned her head slightly side to side. "Sounds a lot like a calf, maybe a lost calf or something coming from that dead elm. way over there."

As they rode closer to the dead tree, the ears of their mounts were locked onto the sounds. When the calf-like bellow paused, the "whoosh" sound of the hooves parting the thick grass and brush became noticeable. Unknown to the two of them, the grass concealed some old fencing which the bay ran into. Luckily, they were riding parallel to the line when the bay clipped a strand of the wire with one of her horse shoes. The iron shoe created a clearly discernable, crisp metallic "click," whereupon Jewel immediately noticed that Sandy began to "high-step."

Jewel had no time to look down on either side. In an instant, the bay bolted to the left and away from the taller brown grass and the fence and into Cantry and Storm. The girl's experience allowed her to quickly regain control of the mare and calm her down, though the mare lifted her head several times trying to fight the reins. The whites of the mare's eyes showed as she looked down and continued to blow through her now enlarged nostrils.

"The heck's goin' on?" Cantry exclaimed.

"Sandy just stepped on a fence wire or metal, something

like that. She spooked at the sound of her horse-shoe clacking on it and…" Jewel's attention went back to the mare.

That, is when the young man noticed two forgotten and forlorn fence posts, just barely poking out of the tall dead grass and weeds. "Jeepers!" he exclaimed. "I didn't even see those posts…I didn't know there was any fence left out here," he said realizing their good fortune of not running into the trap of wire. Jewel dismounted and checked the mare's hooves, fetlocks and legs to make quite sure that no wire had snagged them. Cantry also dismounted.

When she was satisfied there were no injuries she said reassuringly, "Sandy's fine."

Cantry stood and replied with a smile, "So's Storm."

Both mounted and headed towards the sound which seemed to come from a massive dead elm about 200 yards off. As they approached, they could see the base of the elm was cluttered with sheets of bark and a pile of limbs. What they saw next was movement within the clutter. It was a young steer that was not so lucky.

"Well, there's one." Cantry said with mixed emotion.

Both dismounted and approached slowly, giving the frightened, white-eyed steer time to get used to their presence. It was apparent that the back, left leg was caught; stomach deep in the lower squared portion of some legal line fencing. Its front leg wrapped hopelessly in some of the upper barbed wire of the same fence.

"Poor thing. Can we do anything…Cantry?"

"Huhhh," came a sigh, "we'll try to untangle it."

Jewel looked over her left shoulder at the mare whose reins she still clutched. Then she caught something out of the corner of her eye. It was in the distance down by a clump of brush under some cottonwood trees. It was a movement in the shade of the trees. She turned to stare more intently, focusing on the area.

"What is it?" questioned Cantry, half mumbling as he strode over to his gelding and retrieved his rifle, ready to cock the lever and thus chamber a live shell.

"I don't know, I saw something…

"Yeah, I could tell…"

"..Oh, it's a cow!"

Yeah, and another one too, hey," the young man chimed in.

"They sure didn't get very far from this hurt one." She said. Just then the trapped steer let out a loud series of bellows, which was answered very quickly by the other cattle in a cacophony of bellows.

"Funny we didn't hear 'em before," he remarked as he gently and partially opened the receiver to assure himself he had not chambered a shell out of habit. He clasped the lever shut, rubbed the shiny brass receiver with his sleeve and then re-inserted his rifle into the scabbard. "Yep. Stayed within ear-shot." Cantry said approvingly

The mare and the gelding watched also as the cattle one by one came out of the cotton woods and peered up over the rise.

"I count nine, Jewel. What did you get?"

"Ten."

"Alright then," he counted again. "Ten."

"Nine." Came her reply. "What? They keep moving." She proffered as she shrugged her shoulders.

Simultaneously they both turned to the other and suggested in unison, "Well, let's go see."

As they rode closer to the herd, both counted ten, and then promptly returned to the trapped steer to study the situation more closely.

It was difficult to get-in close to the steer as it was surrounded and enmeshed in the dead limbs and tall brush. After some time of looking up and down, underneath and around the steer; Cantry approached at the front. He gave the animal time to smell him. Its left leg, wrapped in wire was planted hoof down in a slight depression. The right leg was free of wire, but bent at the knee, resting on the sod as a support. Cantry had retrieved the fencing pliers from the wallet, but studied the scene. He followed, with his eyes, the two strands of barbed wire through the maze of legs, in between posts and amongst the limbs. He took a deep breath, held it a second and then let it out. Slowly he approached the panting, wide-eyed steer, all the while speaking in a low gentle tone.

After slowly pushing one strand down and out of the way, his hand started on the other strand of barbed wire. The steer, feeling the lessening tension began to jitter and jerk and with that Cantry scooted back a bit on his butt and hands, but quickly gained his feet underneath his legs.

"Whoa, easy, easy, easy eeeeasy…eeeeasy," he continued in a low steady tone.

A few feet behind him came a whisper, "Can you get it?" her light soft tone held the anxiety of not wanting to disturb the steer which had stopped its writhing.

Cantry, not speaking, slowly nodded his head affirmatively while keeping his eyes trained on the steer. He pushed the wire towards the hoof loosening its grip. The loop on the hoof widened slowly until it was a good ten inches in diameter. The steer remained still. Cantry waited and waited. The steer remained immobile while Cantry held the loop open.

"Well c'mon now ya…get up and out," he said in an urgent manner through closed jaws.

Again from behind him Jewel's voice in a hushed tone sounded a warning, "you'd better be careful."

He faintly muttered to himself, "Be careful she says." His

body was noticeably overextended and he knew it. Both of his knees were on the ground, his body leaning well forward. Braced by his left hand and the right outstretched even farther yet. Jumping up quickly was not an option at this point. Cantry slowly backed off on his hands and knees with a different idea. In a steady voice he remarked in a jesting tone to Jewel, "Say, don't yell so much."

She calmly replied back in a loud whisper, "I'm just trying to help."

At a comfortable distance, he stood up and looked around for a long dry branch. Finding one, he then pulled out his toma-hawk and proceeded to trim the end.

Jewel studied his actions and asked, "you need a saw?"

"Yeah, but I'm just trying to make due."

"Wait. I think I can help." She quickly retrieved the multi tool from her pack, and upon unfolding it produced an aggressive saw-blade from amongst the accessories.

"Yeah, That's the ticket," as he took several steps to grasp the tool. He quickly and neatly trimmed off the broken end, after which he sawed a slit across the face of the cut. He looked at the tool ap-provingly before laying it on the ground and said quietly, "I gotta get me one of these." With his tomahawk, he split the wood to open the slit a bit farther, while still allowing the wood to spring shut. He looked at his handiwork, a sort of a long pincer he hoped would work.

He again approached the steer and pushed the open end of the slit limb against the wire to force it into the crack. He was able to open up the loop; this time at a safe distance. The steer feeling the abrupt difference in the tension kicked its leg up and out of the strand which Cantry then yanked away from the leg.

In a series of jerks and bucks the steer regained its stand-ing position. Using the pole for the same purpose Cantry aided the steer in clearing its hind leg of the fencing. It bounced forward awkwardly like a three legged dog and bellowed as it did so. One cow immediately bellowed back.

Jewel retrieved her multi-tool and looked up several times as she folded it closed. "Oh, he's not walking the right way."

"He's probably just stiff," came the reply.

"I…I…I don't think so, it's like he's goin' to fall down," she said slowly shaking her head.

Cantry approached from the rear of the steer causing it to bounce some more. He softly swore as he noticed the lower right hind leg trailing in an awkward position. "He's busted!" came a disappointed exclamation.

"His leg's broke?" came the question in a mournful tone. As she asked this the calf abruptly and ungracefully flopped itself down.

"Yeah or out of joint, or something. Just leave him and we'll have to think of a way to get a hold of Uncle Ian, cause I sure don't know how we could possibly walk him out'a here, and; he's probably going to want to put him down." Cantry stood for a while in silent thought then continued "Ahhhh, I don't know. Uncle Ian, I think, went to town and doesn't have a CB radio in the car. Umm, I s'pose we'll have to give it a try anyway."

Both retrieved their walkie-talkies and attempted to make contact with the base station at the house. However, it was either turned off or no one was home.

CHAPTER FOUR

A Real Cook-out

When no one answered back on the radios, Cantry and Jewel discussed what they would do to contact Uncle Ian. It was decided that Jewel would ride all the way back to the farm, if necessary, and get Ian. A few minutes later Jewel was off to get Ian and so Cantry would stay behind to keep the strays collected in the stand of cottonwoods and keep watch over the injured steer. On the way back, Jewel had been riding for about half-an-hour when she came to the top of a rise and took a rest in the breeze. As she was about to mount-up, she heard a whistle. She looked around and could see only hillocks with brush and grass and the left-saddle fender right in front of her face. She mounted and on her right about a quarter of a mile away, on the next prominent rise, sat Ian on his horse, Crow Wing, or simply "Winger" as he often called him. But there was also someone else on horseback with what looked like a long skinny board across the saddle pommel. They helloed loudly, waved, and then rode towards Jewel and she toward them. As she approached, she watched Ian as he communicated on the short-wave radio, he kept with him. She recognized the other rider as Mark, sitting astride of Abigail, another horse owned by Ian. Mark was a former rodeo cowboy and friend of the family.

"Hello Jewel."

"Mr. Thorvig…Mark, what are you guys doin' out here? I thought you were headin' into town."

"We came looking for you." Said Ian with a grin on his face. "I can go to town later, sometime. Did you try to raise me on the radio?"

"Yep, we tried. D'ya think we were lost?"

"No, That's not it, I s'pose I just needed an excuse to go riding." Confessed Ian.

"Where d'ya pick him up at?" Jewel asked playing into the banter of the moment. "Say, you're pretty decked out like a trapper or mountain man or..."

"Metis [3]," returned Mark, 'the coat I'm wearing is a Metis coat made from brain tanned deer skins that I made and painted. The buckskin leggin's are Metis too."

"MAY-tee?" Jewel said quizzically.

"Yeah, Indian and French or Indian and Scot. It's the same as saying mixed blood."

"Oh, okay." Then Jewel leaned forward on her stirrups to exclaim, "And you got...spurs on your moccasins?" then she emphasized, "Moccasins?"

"Yep," Mark retorted, "just like in the Miller [4] paintings. "

Ian suddenly broke into the conversation, "Well anyways, Mark came over to do some shooting with his black powder rifle and me with my pistol. I had asked him about some clothing so he just figured he'd just wear some and show me that way. He didn't have any idea that the cattle had gotten out. So, instead of scrappin' time meant for shooting, I talked him into goin' with me on horseback and just take our guns along with us. I strapped on my Forty-four revolver and he took along his flintlock rifle and his Paterson [5] pistol, and some other stuff he had in the truck. He's 'batching it' this week. We tried to get you on the radio, but there was no reply."

"Yep, I got nowhere to be this week," Mark interjected as he pointed to the back of his saddle, "So, I grabbed my wool capote [6] and my haversack and other stuff and got acquainted with Abigail here."

Jewel surveyed Mark's outfit "Oh yeah." She then changed the subject, "Ya' know, Cantry has got his gun...er rifle; the Henry.

Besides we might need to use a gun 'cause we found one of the steers and he banged up his leg by getting tangled in some old fencing. We freed him. Actually, Cantry cut him loose, but he's hurt. It's sort of dragging and um, Cantry thinks it's busted."

"Front...Back?" quizzed Ian

"Back," confirmed Jewel, as she watched Ian swear under his breath.

"You sure?

"Pretty darn..." Jewel shot back, "it won't stay standing."

The two men tuned to look at each other; their heads slightly nodded downward, eyebrows lifted, and lips pushed down as if to silently say, 'Oh really?'

"Pretty good call Ian." Said Mark, patting the pistol in its holster near the pommel and then quickly moving his arm to point at Ian's pistol.

Jewel picked up on the gesture and wanted in on the thought, "What? What is it?"

"Well, I was considering," Ian began, "a barbeque after talking with Mr. Jordhiem. I was just mulling the idea of slaughtering a steer and using a part of that for a cook-out. And then Mark reminded me, after he arrived, that the Fargo club is havin' their black powder rendezvous this coming weekend." He paused for a moment. "On Jordhiem's property, only I was hoping to choose the steer, not have it chosen for me." He grinned as he shook his head. "What can you do?" he commented in a cynical tone and was met with shrugging shoulders and smirks from both Mark and Jewel.

Jewel tried to reassure him, "We can still make the best of it." She paused, "Ya' know, we were just talking about that same subject; whether Curty and Sinster were gonna do that same sort'a deal this summer."

"Say," interrupted Ian, "I called around to see if anyone had seen the cattle. When I talked to one of the Lynnes boys, he said those three dogs are still running loose and this morning he and Mr. Erickson chased them out of his sheep, not far from here on some land he's leasing. Said they headed down towards uh…Sam Vangsness' place." He paused for a moment. "That's not too awfully far from here, anyway."

"Yeah, well we came across one dead steer in a coulee and Cantry shot a dog that must have been injured in the kill. It was a bloody mess. Otherwise we haven't seen any other dogs for that matter anywhere while we've been riding."

"Coyotes?" asked Mark.

"None that we've seen." Returned Jewel as she stared between the two of them.

Ian and Mark simply nodded. Both were deep in thought. Mark looked down at the ground; his tongue shifted around the Copenhagen in his lip. He looked up at Ian who was also unconsciously doing the same with his own "snoose."

"Well, I s'pose we maybe should get going, so's I can get back before the end of the day." Ian said in a restless manner.

Mark replied, "Well, alright then, let's get to it."

With Jewel leading the way, the trio headed towards Cantry and the cattle. As they rode Ian asked about the rest of the cattle and Jewel fleshed out the encounter near the dead calf, then explained the injured steer and the rest of the cattle and the gave him a good report at which point Ian cracked a short-lived smile that was tempered with melancholy.

"Say…" began Jewel, "how'd you guys get out here so fast?"

Ian began with a chuckle, "I guess it started when Mr. G-Ray Tolsruud stopped by to ask about some of last fall's hay bales still in the ditch and he was pulling an empty horse trailer. So, I asked if he was doing anything for a little while and he said 'yeah,' but that if we needed a lift, he could maybe give us a hand. I think he put two and two together when he saw our two horses saddled up. So, we came in from the north on 23. He trailered us to the horse camp. We made our way south on the trails and kept on turning west and finally I figured we had better head east somewhat or else we were going to end up on that next road back to the north. We've been cutting east-southeast for about a quarter-hour. We almost missed you!"

"Ok then, how did you know to start there? Jewel replied incredulous at the luck of their choice.

"G Ray," Ian said quickly, "He was headin' south on 18 when said he saw you two, or at least two riders heading across that CRP and into the grasslands. He happened to tell me what he saw 'cause he figured it was a couple of riders from the horse camp that had gotten way off track and… Say, you must have gone north of those three shelter belts and…"

"Um, we actually went in between 'em and kept heading west. There were cow pies on the road so we headed in; right there."

"Well, G Ray must have seen you before you hit the trees on the other side of the clearing." he looked at Jewel as if stunned. "JEEEPERS!" Ian suddenly exclaimed, "What in the heck was pushing those cattle so far and so fast. Jiminie Christmas man!"

Jewel could only look back her head quickly nodding say, "I know, I know, right. Cantry thinks they were trying to stay in open areas where it would be hard to sneak up on 'em."

"Kind'a like buffalo; staying in the open where they're harder to approach," responded Mark.

When the three finally reached Cantry, they quickly got down to business. After exchanging greetings, they jumped into a discussion about what to do with the steer; whether to dispatch it and get a tractor, or how to get it out. Cantry did not want to leave

45

it after having gone to all the trouble of finding the herd and un-
tangling the steer from the fencing. Ian had a good idea of the lay
of the land since he and Mark came in from a known road and Ian
also had a mental map from having flown over the area numerous
times. They could dispatch the animal, quarter it and pack it out
to the nearest graveled-maintenance road that lay about two miles
or more straight to the west. They would have a good trail, for at
least, half the way there. The rest of the way would be open ground.
Parallel to the road, was a fordable coulee that lay in the way and
probably filled with water, but it could be followed to the south until the coulee became shallow enough to cross through it. The only
problem was covering the meat.

"You sure you want to do this, Cantry" Ian queried, "I
mean, it is going to be a lot of dog-gone work. If we don't get done
it could mean a night under the stars."

"Dogs or no dogs, are you ready for an adventure?" Mark
barked out with a grin showing in the middle of a rather thick
beard. "I'd stay out here with Cantry, if that would help."

Cantry looked at Mark with a determined look but said
nothing about the "dog" comment. With his jaw set forward and
front teeth clenched together, he emphatically replied, "YES! I want
to do this, and yes I will stay out here, if need be."

Uncle Ian then asked Jewel, "I think I'm going to send Abigail with you as a pack horse, if you don't mind?

Jewel, quickly responded, "Heck no. I don't mind.

"Hey Mark," Ian shouted, "You mind if she takes Abby?"

"Nope." came the reply, "She's all yours."

"Ok then. We are going to need meat bags. Jewel, can you
ride straight west of here starting with that trail we crossed? I
believe it curves from south to west and if you follow it, you'll run
right up to that coulee. The road is just on the other side of the cou-

lee. If it's filled with water, follow it south until you can cross. You can meet Ma there." Ma was Ian's pet name for his wife Barb. "I'll see if I can raise her on my radio and have her go get some game bags so we can pack the meat."

It took ten minutes on the radio to finally catch Barb. It took another ten minutes to explain to her about butchering the calf. Though Barb did not seem "sold" on the idea, she never-the-less accepted it. Ian told her where to find the meat bags, and cheese cloth. Before he was done with the request, he quickly added, "Ma, we also need several pieces of canvas from the garage."

Barb's voice came back, "So you want meat bags, cheese cloth and canvas? And you're sure about this?"

"Yah, yah we are, and the canvas is by the door nearest to the potato cellar. Uhh... wait a second.."

Mark was waiving his hands over his head to catch Ian's attention and as soon as Ian un-keyed the mic he asked, "As long as she's coming out here see if she can grab the blanket in my truck; its white with a black stripe at either end."

Ian put the radio to his mouth, "Yah, Ma, Mark wants you to grab his white wool blanket too. It's in his truck."

As they waited, time seemed to drag and finally Ian received a beep and a voice,

"Ok, I've got the meat bags, cheese cloth and some pieces of canvas; and Mark's blanket. That's a nice piece of wool. It seems a shame to get it dirty, but then again if he wants it that bad I'll have it with. I assume someone is spending the night?" There was a long pause and then she spoke up, "Ok then, I'm gonna head down the gravel road that goes south of that farm along the Sheyenne. I'll meet Jewel on that road about a mile south of the farm. Looking at the map it looks like there's a sharp curve. But, before I get to the..." Barb paused to study the map, "I should not go past the curve? Is that right?"

Ian quickly responded, "Oh yah, that's right. By golly, there is a fairly tight curve there. Yeah, I'll draw Jewel a map. She says she'll meet you there."

"Hey, how's about water and some buckets?" Barb quickly threw out the question.

Ian turned to the others and said, "See, that's why I love that woman, she's always thinking of the important stuff." He put the radio back to his mouth and with a big grin confirmed, "Yeah, water, and buckets tha' twould be nice. If the short tank on the truck is full get a bunch of jugs too." He waited for perhaps another great idea from Barb and finally he finished, "Ok Ma, 10-4."

"Yep, 10-4 and out."

In no time Jewel was on her mare. She removed her blanket, tossed it to Cantry and with Abigail in tow, she headed for the meeting point. Ian and Mark flipped a coin to see who would dispatch the injured steer. Mark got the toss and so he retrieved the iron mounted southern style rifle from one of the trees where the rifle had been leaning, then headed over to face the steer. With the shooting pouch that hung from his side he grabbed the stopper of the horn with his teeth and trickled some FFg [7] into the pan of the lock and shut the frizzen. Mark then advanced to positioned himself for the shot. Ian stood to the left of Mark so he would not be hit from the spray spitting from the touch-hole.[8] Ian had removed his own black powder revolver from its cross-draw holster and now it hung pendulously in his right hand pointed down where it could be brought to bear as a back-up for Mark.

Mark brought the lock to full-cock, squeezed the set trigger,[9] and as soon as he had placed an imaginary "X" on the steer's head he touched the front trigger. BOOOM!

Though Ian was ready to follow through, if needed, one shot

from the .54 flinter and it was all over. The other cattle jumped a little, but did not run. Cantry, who had mounted Storm, had by this time removed the lariat from his saddle, his right hand gripped the spoke and the honda[10], ready to lasso the steers head. As soon as Mark had moved away from the steer, Cantry swung the lariat overhead and lassoed the steer's head.

Mark looked up at Cantry and jokingly said, "Show-off!"

Cantry said nothing but smiled at Mark. Storm seeing the lariat around the steer's head instinctively began to back up until it was taut and waited for Cantry's direction.

Ian, on the other hand, walked over to the steer and placed his own lariat on the steer's head then walked back and mounted Winger. With lariats around the dead steer's neck, Ian, on Crow-Wing and Cantry on Storm, dragged the steer into the shade of some near-by trees. Ian produced his lock-blade, Mark his sheath knife with an antler handle and Cantry, now in good company, unsheathed his belt-knife as well. The three men went to work, eviscerated the steer, removed the hide from one side. The steer was rolled back onto the open hide and the unskinned side was opened up as well.

With the meat exposed, they removed the front shoulder, hind quarter and back-straps, and continued to bone-out the rest. They laid the pieces on the open hide until Mark could get some strips cut from the edge of the steer hide to use in place of rope.

As soon as he had cut two eight-foot pieces he then cut these down to four footers. In the ends of these strips he poked holes and inserted short, stout sections of a branch which would act as a stop to keep the knots in the slippery hide from slipping through. In this manner Mark, with Cantry's help, began to hang the large quarters from nearby trees. With each one he made sure the fresh hide-thongs held their knots and thus kept the meat off the ground.

"Well," Ian began, "I s'pose I should have brought some extra rope, meat bags and canvas in my saddle bags."

Mark replied, "If your bags are that big you would be pretty well healed." Mark paused for a second, then added, "Say, since you have extra room in your saddle bags, you wouldn't happen to have a fridge in them would you, with maybe a cold beer in it?"

Ian puffed out a quick sigh as he smiled and answered, "Nope, but I can sure give you a "cold one" when we get home or maybe at the rendezvous this weekend."

Cantry offered, "Hey, Mark, Jewel still has a warm soda in her saddle bag, if you're interested. There's hot dogs too, that is when she gets back she can get 'em for you."

Mark looked up from the meat for a second to say, "Warm soda isn't quite the same a cold beer, unless there's a wee bit to mix with it." He then changed the subject to ask Ian about the horses packing fresh meat.

Ian's response was to lift his head and as he turned to Cantry he said, "Hey, take 'n lead Storm down wind of where we're butchering so's he'll get used to the smell of fresh meat and blood. I'm not so worried about my horse but I don't know if your horse or Marks is blood-broke."

Cantry responded, "you mean like horses on an elk hunt?"

"Yep, that would be the ticket," answered Ian nodding his head. "We'll probably do the same with Abby and Sandy when Jewel gets back with them."

Cantry led Storm down wind of the butchering and then closer to the site where he stood holding the reins to see if he would shy or outright spook. After a short time he lead him off and back again. When Storm became restless or anxious with the scene Cantry spoke to him calmly as the gelding tried to turn away. He answered these gestures by turning him in circles to face the butchering area again, and had him stand until he was calm.

When most of the meat was quartered, boned and hung, the three began to wash their hands with the water from their canteens. As they did so Ian spotted what looked like a ring of rocks, which was peculiar because this area was almost all sand; hence, locals referred to it as the "Sand Hills". Wanting to satisfy his curiosity, he walked to the ring, spread the grass and leaves and lo, he found a fire-pit with some ashes which he grabbed up. Using a little more water, he rubbed the grey ash over his hands like soap and then had Cantry rinse it off little by little with Ian's canteen water. It worked fairly well, he thought. There must be enough lye left in the ashes [11] to cut the tallow and meat juices. He showed Mark and Cantry the ashes in the fire ring and they did likewise.

Next on the agenda was to build a small smokey fire, to keep the flys away. Since there was already a fire ring, most of the meat was hung around and near the ring.

"Keep an eye on the wind," remarked Ian to Mark. "I know it's damp, but we don't need a prairie fire."

"Yep, good idea," reassured Mark, "the pocket where you found that fire ring, seems to be pretty well protected. We could "make smoke" until dusk. Maybe, if we cool down some cuts from the back-straps, we could even cook a little yet before evening." Mark, who was sporting a large smile, had lifted his head and cast his comment directly at Ian.

Cantry jumped in on the comment, "Oh yah, too bad there wasn't some root beer and corn on the cob to go along with the meat."

With that Ian stood up to watch Mark and Cantry. He noticed that Mark was cutting small saplings and branches and making a rack. He bellowed at Mark, "You serious about cooking some

51

meat?"

"Sure, the tenderloins or the cuts off of the rump could be cooked up pretty fast," quipped Mark.

"Naw!" came the reply from Ian.

"What the heck, why not?" questioned Cantry. "We're going to be here waiting for Jewel to get back with the bags and stuff. Are you goin' to try and get the cattle outta here before dark? 'Cause I don't think you have enough time for the meat and the cattle. That's why I plan to stay and make camp, Mark too."

"You guys, by the time we cook up some meat it will be time to leave! Cantry you have hot dogs. Well, Jewel does anyway..."

"Ian," Mark gently interrupted as he explained his thoughts to Ian, "I'm going to start a fire and create some smoke. I'll watch it and make sure it doesn't go anywhere. While I'm at it, I'll take a few small cuts, nothing that you'll even miss. I'll build up the coals for heat, and, in no time, I'll have something we can all eat. It'll probably be cooked before Jewel gets back with the hot dogs. How's about that?" Mark held his breath while he waited for Ian's reply.

Ian paused for a moment, "well, we could try. I s'pose though, it all depends on when Barb gets to where Jewel can meet her and..." his voice trailed off as he began to consider the logistics of the cattle. "Yah, well...my trailer only holds five or so cattle and...dang it! Too bad we didn't have G Ray down here with his trailer too, we could probably have all the cattle out in one trip. Ahh, shoot! Ma's already on her way and has no way to phone G-Ray." Ian muttered another epithet under his breath.

"Well," Cantry slowly edged in his comment, "uh, those ten cattle are worth more than the one we got hangin' and ..."

"Yep," interjected Mark, "I'm already committed to watch the meat and the fire, and stay the night. Everyone else can drive the cattle to the west. Besides, it's been a while since I cut out a steer. So, Cantry! Is Storm a good herd horse?"

"Oh, heck yah Storm loves to push cows. He's better than a Border Collie." Cantry said confidently. "But how do we get ahold of G Ray and his trailer?" he said as he raised his hand and waived at Uncle Ian.

Mark slapped his thigh as he stood up, "Good it's settled, I'll stay and you guys can drive."

"I'm still not sure," said Ian, as he looked directly at Mark. "I s'pose we'll have to wait until Barb meets up with Jewel, and…" Ian was a bit exasperated. With a quick head-bob he exclaimed, "Ahh, heck of a deal!" As a pilot and a farmer Ian was usually thinking way ahead. "Well, if we don't do it tonight, then ahh,… We're going to have to take watches and keep an eye on the cattle." With that he paused for a moment and then uttered again in a low voice, "Yep, heck of deal."

Cantry meandered over to the tree where he has placed the wallet after untying it. The walkie-talkie was lying on top. He picked up the radio and walked over to Storm and out of nervousness he checked on the saddle and began to pet the horse's neck. He hoped that maybe Jewel would have her radio on too; even though nobody mentioned it. He stood by his horse as he keyed the mic'.

"Hey Jewel, you got a copy? Hey Jewel, this is Cantry, you got a copy?" He stood silently by the gelding with his head tilted down waiting for a response. His eyes darted around anxiously. He placed his right hand on his hip, a sign of some impatience. He repeated the call.

At this Ian's ears perked up and he walked across the glade until he came around Cantry's gelding. He motioned silently with his left hand, and Cantry, catching his movement out of the corner of his left eye turned to face Uncle Ian. Then, seeing the gesture, he walked over to his uncle. The two stood there waiting for a response for several minutes, at which point Uncle Ian offered a suggestion.

"Let's leave that on for a while. As long as you don't key the mic', it shouldn't drain the battery." With that, Cantry reached down pulled up a stem of grass, and as he put it in his mouth, looked at Uncle Ian who simply nodded in agreement.

Across the glade, Mark who was kneeling at the ring of rocks, had taken out his flint and steel from a small belt pouch and began to strike at his flint to begin the process of making a fire. Ian and Cantry could hear Mark striking away, *chick… chick, chick, chick, chick,* the oval shaped piece of steel in Mark's right hand came down to scrape the flint in Mark's left hand, the sparks from the striker rolled up and backward, away from the edge to land on the charcloth, and, just then, one of the sparks caught in the soft black cloth…suddenly there was an orange dot.[12]

Mark blew on the char-cloth to reveal a hot glow, then let it slide from the top of the flint into a small nest of tinder he had made from grass and dried cottonwood fibers. He used the edge of the flint to maneuver the orange and black mass into the center of the tinder where he had placed a bit of loose linen tow [13] which he had retrieved from his brass tinder box. He began to blow, *Whooooooo,* followed by a breath-in *Huhh-* and another blow at the tinder, *Whooooo.* Mark blew steadily, took in a quick breath and then blew steadily, *Huhhh-Whooooo.* The smoke began to collect around his hands as the glowing char singed the tinder. Another breath in and out, *Huhh-Whooooo,* and again, *Huhhh-Whooooo.* Soon smoke inundated the tinder nest until…suddenly a flame appeared. He lowered the burning bundle and gently pushed it under the small crisscross raft of twigs which supported a small "log-cabin" affair of more dry sticks and twigs.

"Well, by-golly, that stuff worked pretty good," uttered Ian who watched the flames begin to grow. And just as soon as the words were out of his mouth a voice came across Cantry's radio.

"Hey Cantry you got your ears on?" it was Jewel.

Cantry who had been holding the radio, but totally en-grossed in Mark's efforts, jumped at the sound of the voice in his hands. At which point he removed the stem of grass in his jaws, took a breath, and spit as he raised the radio to his face.

"Yah, this is Cantry. Come-on back."

"Hey 'good lookin' tell your Uncle Ian that Barb is right here, she brought the stuff. Abby and I are all loaded up with bags, cloth and canvas, water buckets and Mark's blanket."

"Ahhh, for nice! That didn't take too long," Cantry said a bit giddy.

"Nope, and you'll never guess what else..."

Cantry lost his smile; assuming that something may have gone wrong. "What is it?" he asked in a serious tone.

Jewel did not answer immediately and when she did, she began sounding a bit uncertain, "Well, um, Barb was headin' over here and she came across none other than, G Ray, who, was load-ing hay into his trailer, and he asked about you guys. So, Barb told him that you'd found the cows, but one needed to be butchered, and that no one had said anything about bringing the rest of 'em in. Then, just like that, he offered to help if it was this evening. He said he's got today and tomorrow free, but after that he'll be unavailable. How's about that?"

Cantry and Ian sat there a bit stunned at their good fortune and his facial expression relaxed. Ian's mind was in a totally differ-ent set of thoughts. He knew what Barb would do. She would say, "It's a God thing, Perfect timing." and then smile and go about her chores. At that point Ian reached for the walkie-talkie to retrieve it from Cantry's hand.

"Hey Jewel, this is Ian... is G Ray offering to bring his

trailer?

"Hey Mr. Thorvig, uh, that's what it sounded like when she, I mean, Barb talked to him. And he…Just a minute." the conversation halted as it seemed that Jewel was conferring with Barb.

The next voice that came from the receiver was Barb, "Hey Dear. Yeah G Ray sounded like he could have a mount ready and bring him with. He sounded like he was lookin' for an excuse to herd some cattle with his horse, but…" she paused for a few seconds before she continued, "he said ah, he said that if he's eating dinner or supper he wants to finish eating, 'cause he doesn't want to have no," she broke into a giggle, "…doesn't want no "skin on his gravy." Barb broke into a full laugh as it was one of the phrases that G Ray was known for using in reference to cold soup or gravy.

Ian waited for a few seconds as he too was laughing a bit as he waited for Barb to un-key the mic.

He returned his answer, "Yah, well that sounds great. Tell G Ray whenever he wants to get down here with his trailer tha'twould be fine. Say…he could probably help you with our trailer as well… so maybe that's a possibility too."

Barb returned her receipt of the suggestion, "oh yah, we could probably get both trailers down there and have those cows at least to the trailers before it turned full dark…maybe. Hey, why can't you guys just try him, he's on channel 23."

"I don't have channel 23." Cantry answered as he looked at Ian, "I have the crystals for 9, 11, 17, 19 and 40."

Ian spoke, "Yeah, but Cantry doesn't have that channel."

"Oh, ok, Ahh… I get you. It seems G Ray's radio dial is stuck on Channel 23. Never mind. I'll see if I can raise him. This is Ma, 10-4 we're out."

With that Ian and Cantry, both smiling, walked over to the fire that Mark was building for cooking some of the back-straps or "chops" as he called them. Each man had a stick with two or three pieces of meat at its end and propped it up at the edge of the coals. The cuts were already sizzling. Cantry sat down with the radio between his feet and simply stared at his cuts of meat.

"Well…" started Ian with a satisfied grin, "I s'pose as long as were here we might as well have us a little cook-out."

Suddenly a voice came from between Cantry's feet and he jumped at the sound. "Ah, Naaman, I got to quit flinching like that." He picked up the radio, "Yah, what is it?

"Well, G Ray wanted to know if you were cooking that butchered steer and I told him I would ask. He said if you were cooking it, he would bring some salt and pepper and wants to know if you want some cold refreshment."

Cantry quickly handed the radio to Ian. "Hey Ma, tell him, heck yah, we're cooking some meat and it looks like a couple of these guys are going to spend the evening here at camp if we don't get the meat to the truck, cause I'm more interested in getting those cattle out than I am tending to this meat….." Ian knew he was going down a rabbit hole of how to administer the operation and he stopped himself and began again. "Yah, tell G Ray we're cooking meat and there's some here who would be appreciative of some cold refreshment." Ian who had broken into a wry grin, looked to Mark who had heard the description that Ian had emphasized. Mark gave Ian a "thumbs-up."

No answer came for a few minutes as all three men were looking up at the sky and making small talk as to horses and running cattle. And just as quickly the radio cracked with some static and Barb's voice, "Yah, ok Dear, G Ray says he's on his way, but you'd better have some meat ready for him."

"Yeah, well thanks for that good news. Tell G Ray we'll have plenty of meat and he can choose whether he wants well-done, medium, or some form of rare…but no skin." Ian's face stretched into his mischevous grin with the last comment as he began to chuckle.

"Okay, 10-4"

"Yah, 10-4 and out." Ian handed the radio back to Cantry.

By this time, some of the meat was cooked and each man began to pull off a piece of cooked chop, blowing on it to cool it down and shifting it from hand to hand. Mark leaned to one side, reached into a small pouch that was not all that noticeable and pulled out a small horn with a stopper and began to salt his cooked beef. Without a word he handed the horn to the other two and they salted theirs as well. The horn was handed back. All sat and chewed, swallowed, chewed, swallowed followed by more chewing and swallowing.

As they sat there eating and rearranging meat on the various leaning spits, Jewel's voice came on the radio to say that she and G-Ray were on their way and would be there in about twenty minutes. Cantry mumbled to himself, "Well, that makes sense. She's leading him back to our position. I was wondering why she hadn't gotten back yet."

After what seemed only seconds but was probably more like several minutes a shot was heard straight to the west. At the sound, all the men looked at each other with quizzical but serious looks.

Cantry spoke first, "What do ya' s'pose that was for?"

Mark stood straight, his back erect and said nothing but turned his head in small jerks one way only a few degrees and then back again. He spit as he started towards Cantry and said, "I wonder if they saw a coyote or something, maybe he's shooting at a gopher? Who knows? Maybe it's a signal that they're on their way back." Mark sat back down and reached for another piece of meat which he ate eagerly.

CHAPTER FIVE

Back at Camp

It was barely fifteen minutes after the sound of a shot pierced the evening when they heard G Ray's voice, "Helloooo the camp!"

Cantry quickly whistled and answered, "HO! Come on in."

Jewel came in past a row of trees to the south. She, Sandy and Abby cast long shadows in the fading light of day. From her saddle horn she sported four water jugs, two over her left side and two over top of her lariat. She had quite a pile of white and cream-colored cloth on the back of her saddle. It was tied into two different roles. She rode up to a low basswood that was lying horizontally but still alive. As she dismounted, she leaned more forward than usual in order to raise her right leg over the large roles behind her. She cleared her heel and planted her right foot on the tree, then her left. "Whew! We're back."

Jewel then tended to the half-bale of hay and soft-sided three gallon jug on Abby's back, along with two bags of oats.

G Ray rode in on his chestnut, ironically, named Butternut who was festooned with an assortment of canvas, blankets, coat, water jugs, sleeping bag, lariat, and a rifle in a scabbard. G Ray often referred to his mount as "Cow-Nut" ostensibly because the horse seemed to enjoy chasing, herding and even mischievously pestering cows by pawing at them like a dog.

G Ray dismounted and began to remove the newly arrived freight. As he did so the horse stood, his ears were forward, locked in place. He looked intently at the group of cows and pawed the ground once or twice. G Ray, who was sporting his usual western hat and his zip-up leather chaps that he had worn for many years, was dressed for action. He could tell Butternut was also eager for some action, namely, to chase cattle. He spoke calmly to the eager horse, "Soon enough Cow-Nut. Soon enough." He then turned to the rest of the group at the fire ring. "Hey, good to see you guys here. Do you have some meat? My belly is rubbin' my back-bone." His accent was a heavy Norwegian brogue that he had been known for since he was a youngster.

Ian piped up, "Hey, I'd know that Norske voice anywhere."

"Yep," G Ray responded, "My wife always says that they tried to cure me of it, but it failed." And as he finished his statement; he laughed in a quiet, staccato, guttural tone.

Many pleasantries were exchanged, as well as an introduction between Mark and G-Ray, who, addressed Mark, "I s'pose this is your white blanket I been carryin'?" he handed it to Mark who promptly laid it out on his bedding area. After which, G Ray and Jewel sat down to have some roasted cuts of beef. They made small talk for a few minutes when Ian began with a few questions.

"Say…what was that shot we heard just after we got off of the radio?"

Jewel who was still chewing shrugged her shoulders and tilted her head towards G Ray whose eyebrows lifted up and he finally spoke. "Waalll, I seen this coyote skittering trou' d' brush and so I dismounted and tried a poke at him. He was only about fifty-sixty yards off and its dead calm."

"So, d'you get him?"

"Naw. Dust kicked up just in front of him and he went from a trot to an all out run. We didn't dare take the time to go look. I'll look tomorrow when I have a chance, but I'm sure I didn't touch him. Say, we'd better get goin with them cattle, else it's goin' ta' get dark awfully soon."

Ian shot a call over to Mark to assure him, "Hey Mark, if

you wanted to get started covering that meat you could make quite a dent in it. What you don't finish I would think that folks will have enough time to bag up the rest of the meat after coming back."

"All righty!" came Mark's response. "Ian, I'll probably see you tomorrow."

After getting a bite to eat G Ray and Jewel were back in the saddle and before G Ray went any further, he untied his saddle bags and gave them to Ian and said, "You might want to leave this here for now."

Ian peered inside to see two bottles of coke. He reached in and found them ice-cold to the touch and quickly closed the flap and smiled with the comment, "Oh yah." At which point he whistled to Mark to come grab the bags.

The plan had remained the same, that Mark would stay behind with the meat and keep the fire going and the rest, Ian, Cantry, Jewel, and G Ray began to move the cattle towards the trail and the waiting trailers.

With whistles and slapping of lariats, the riders made noise to move the cattle. Ian and Jewel stayed in the rear and kept the cattle moving while Cantry and G Ray kept the roamers in check. On occasion one of them would chase after a steer or cow and direct the animal back to the moving entourage.

Soon Mark could no longer hear the whistles and shouts of the drovers and he sat looking at the fire. As the sun was nearly touching the horizon, something out of the corner of his eye caught his attention. "Was that a dog or a deer?" he thought to himself. If it was a dog or even a coyote, he might like to reconnoiter the land within a hundred yards about camp. If something got wind of the fresh meat it would be too much to resist. Though there was not really much of a breeze, the smell of blood seemed to carry a long way. Any preditor from weasel to bear would be able to sniff the air and follow it. Not that there were any bear in the area, but there were coyotes and other meat eaters like coon and badgers and such.

Mark quickly re-loaded his .54 flinter with 70 grains of FFg and then put the patching [14] into his mouth to moisten with spit [15] while he retrieved a round ball from his pouch. With the round ball placed on the patch and over the muzzle he slapped it down with the pommel of his knife. He drove the ball all-the-way-home [16] with his ram rod and upon replacing the rod he primed the pan of the lock and climbed aboard Abby.

His first move was to travel somewhat with the wind to the east then cut south and investigate any little pockets, holes or even dens that may lie close to camp. His little sortie took about fifteen minutes and when he returned to camp he unsaddled and unbridled Abby to feed in a patch of new grass. He left her halter on with the lead rope tied to a tree. He thought about the rope that Jewel had brought back with her to be used as a high line picket for the horses. He studied the area for it a few minutes amid the gro-ing shadows and, when he located what he was looking for, he tied one end of the rope to a convenient tree and stretched it through an open area to attach to another tree. Although not totally up the middle of the glade, it was far enough away from several trees that it would allow the horses to move without getting lead ropes tan-gled around other trees. When it was as taut as he could muster, he tied it off. Following that, he tied Abby to it and was satisfied that the rope would allow good use of the glade. After building up the fire again he proceeded to grab a jug of water and wash his hands.

He secured a small scrap of clean cloth in the bundle of can-vas and meat bags and used it to wipe his hands dry, then began the task bagging the hanging meat. As he worked each bag up around a quarter and tied-off the open end just below the branch where the rawhide thong held. All the quarters, save and except for a collection of cuts, were wrapped up as darkness grew closer. The camp looked like a collection of ghosts that were hovering amid the trees. The night was noticeably cool and he was glad he had brought his capote and waistcoat and, thanks to Barb he even had a blanket. He positioned the canvas that Jewel had brought so he could set up at least two lean-tos side by side, around the fire ring. He made ready to camp for the night.

With the last bit of light, he found three relatively stout branches. Two pieces of canvas could each share a pole and with three pieces of small rope and several stakes he began to arrange the lean-to. An ash formed the front cross bar suspended by a pole at either front corner. He used two heavier pieces of rope for the poles at those front corners so they remained taut. He was able to find a long basswood sapling that he used to run from the ground up to the middle of the cross-bar. The basswood sapling supported the canvas and prevented sagging. The canvas pieces overlapped at the sapling like a large shingle. Before he could finish, he found it necessary to stoke up the fire. In the flickering light of the fire, he realized he had run out of small-rope, so he cut small strips of canvas which he twisted for use as ropes to secure the canvas to stakes he pounded into the ground. He fetched his saddle to use for a pillow and the horse blanket he folded out to create a ground cloth of sorts. There was more than enough room for four people. The horses would be easy to view throughout the night. Now the only problem was, who would bring coffee in the morning? Mark laid down to test his bed and it was comfy. He took a couple of swigs from one of the bottles of coke that G Ray had brought in the saddle bags and rested his head on the saddle.

Suddenly, Mark heard voices. His horse whinnied and nickered while the other horses were coming in. Mark realized at that point that he had dozed off. He got up and put a few pieces of wood on the fire and fanned the coals with his hat.

"Any meat left?" came G-Ray's voice. "Maybe something to wash down the trail dust too. Hey, did you have a tent in your back pocket? Man, you've been busy." Cantry and G-Ray, who had rifles, were in the lead with Ian and Jewel behind. The two came up to admire the make-shift lean-to. Cantry was the first to reach Mark and dismount.

"Nope." Mark replied, "just used some of the canvas that you got from Ian's farm."

"Hey, looks like you got the meat covered, mostly?" Cantry said approvingly over his shoulder as he walked towards the hanging meat.

"Yep," Mark replied, "Heart and liver are bagged up too. There's only one collection of meat that needs covering."

Cantry visited the one uncovered collection of cuts and after removing some more meat to roast, used a combination of cheese cloth and bits of canvas to bag and cover it as well. When he was done, he headed to the fireside with everyone else to join in on the conversation and cook his selection of cuts.

Mark had noticed that Jewel was packed with four more jugs of water hanging from her saddle. "Say," Mark began, "I see you brought more water. That could almost end up in a nick-name."

"Yep," replied Ian, "she's our water girl."

"Oh no," came the quip from Jewel, "yer not stickin' me with a nick name like that."

"I was thinking of something more like, Molly Pitcher, a woma…"

"WHO!" Jewel retorted as she cut Mark off in mid sentence.

"Molly Pitcher!" Mark began timidly, "who was a woman that brought water to the troops while her husband did his part on one of the cannon crews. She was at her husband's side at the Battle of Monmouth during the Revolutionary War. When he passed out from heat exhaustion, his wife Molly dropped her water bucket and picked up one of the tools to load the cannon and continued the fight. Molly Hayes, was her full name, I think. Before that fight, she earned the name Molly "Pitcher" because she brought water to everyone. So there you go…Molly." Mark looked straight at Jewel as he finished his dissertation.

No one said anything for a short while.

Jewel looked around at the men who were nodding in approval, except for Cantry who was away from the fire, in the dark standing between the horses. He was clearly discernable with the fire-light that reflected off of his face and hat. He quickly ducked down and then turned away when her eyes met his. He was attempting to avoid any eye contact that she cast at him. She began with tired bit of resolve aimed at Cantry. "Okay, thanks, Mr. 'Knight in Shining Armor' hiding in the dark, behind his 'steed.' Thanks for defending me!"

His voice emanated from the dark "What can I say?" Cantry then peered up over the saddle. "I'm just a dumb ol' cowboy with a mohawk."

"You don't have a mohawk. I was just kidding," she replied, sounding a bit exasperated. "And get rid of that big pouting lip, I can see that too in the fire-light."

"Why shouldn't I have a boo-boo lip? You're not even into historical stuff and you already got a handle. I don't have one yet."

"Handle?" questioned Jewel.

Mark jumped in with a short explanation, "among buck-skinners it's another word for a nick-name."

At this Jewel exhaled, "It looks like that one's gonna stick. Heck of deal."

After some chuckling from the men, Mark related his observations, "I thought I saw something out a-ways, and it was so fast I couldn't tell if it was a dog or deer. It was about fifteen minutes after you left that I thought I saw something, so I took a ride around to get a feel for the land and maybe get eyes on some animal but didn't see anything. Maybe I'm just jumpy. Mark stopped again, mid sentence, "G Ray who's driving your trailer back?"

"Yah well," G Ray piped up, "Barb talked the wife into driving my truck and trailer back and…I'll explain it to you later." He paused, "Before I forget, we seen a couple of large tracks in the sand of the coulee where we crossed. I don't reckon we got any wolves out here so it kinda looks like big dog tracks. At least their up wind from here and maybe won't smell the meat."

"Okay, that's good to know about the dog tracks. Maybe I did see something." As Mark finished his thought, he looked toward the horses, "Say…Ian, I thought you were going to head back with Barb?"

"Naw," responded Ian who was taking off the saddle and bridle along with the other three. "Why should I let you guys have all the fun. Barb has turned out cattle before and like Mr. Tolsruud said, she's got help. Besides, Barb got ahold of Jewel's parents and told them that I'd be here at the camp with you guys so they would be OK with Jewel staying out here." Ian looked over at Cantry who had his hands out with palms turned up, his expression pained.

"Don't see what's the big deal." Cantry blurted out.

Before he could say anything more Ian continued, "I know you two brought your blankets on this ride, but that's only IF you got stuck between a rock and a hard place and had no choice but stay out here over night. The first order of business we addressed was that we figured that Jewel should probably go back tonight but she wouldn't hear of it.

Jewel spoke up, "Yer, darn tootin. No room in the trailers. My horse stays out here, and I'm staying with my horse."

Ian had turned to look at Jewel and now he turned back to address Cantry, "Calling Jewel's parents was the polite thing to do. They need to be kept in the loop too. I agreed to be chaperone. We sure don't want them worrying about her. It's what parent's do."

"Chaperone?" questioned Cantry, "Really? Isn't that kind of..."

"I believe the word you're looking for is old-fashioned!" answered Ian rather sternly as he stared at Cantry.

Cantry immediately caught the abrupt change in his uncle's demeanor and lowered his head submissively. In a timid, agreeable tone, Cantry quickly replied, "old-fashioned works just fine,"

The young man awkwardly glanced up at his uncle and caught his eyes for a second or two. He saw his uncle nodding back agreeably. Nothing more was said on the matter.

Mark who had been on the other side of the fire and wanting to change the subject, looked up at the sky, "You know, with that clear sky I bet there's going to be a heavy dew and cool air. That and a steady breeze should keep the meat cool and so far, I haven't seen any flys or even a mosquito…yet." Then Mark changed the subject to G Ray's rifle. "Hey G Ray, tell me about your rifle. It looks like a Winchester 73 or like it.

"Oh yah, well, I got wind from, Craig Rowe, who lives south of Kindred, that a fella in Horace wanted to sell it. Said, the man had six boxes of ammo but it was loaded with older powder. It puffs out a good cloud of smoke, and don't have much kick. Wa'll, anyways, I brought it along cause it seemed like the thing to do and after all, I di'nt want to handle my scoped .270 on horse-back."

Mark sat there nodding and looked the gun over when G Ray handed it to him. With an approving nod he gave it back and G

Ray who placed the gun next to his own bed roll after checking to see that no shell was chambered in it.

G Ray then asked Mark about the flintlock rifle and Mark reviewed all the relevant items, such as: the double set triggers, the action of the flint against the frizzen, the .012 deep rifling which had one turn in sixty-six inches, the front sight made from a sterling-silver dime, and the tallow hole in the side of the stock. Eventually, G Ray handed the rifle back to Mark who then tied some wool around the lock area to protect it from the evening's moisture. The rifle was then put next to his bed roll.

Jewel, who had been watching the examination of the rifles suddenly asked Mark, "So Mark, what's the draw? I mean, what is it about history that pulls *you* into using the clothing and guns and stuff? Cantry gave me his explanation earlier today, but I just thought I'd ask you."

"Alrighty then," Mark began, "it's neat to use what was used back in-the-day for hunting, camping, cooking, and other activities and get it right. It's more than knowing how to use this flintlock of mine, but it goes to my abilities in being proficient in its use in the field. The same goes for making and wearing clothing. It is sort of a continual sense of accomplishment. Does that make sense?"

"Yeah," Jewel responded quietly, "I don't seem to have that same drive as you and Cantry though."

"OK, you might never have that same drive as Cantry and me, but I think you understand that for someone to portray a certain year in history, the clothing and guns, for instance, should probably match that time period. That takes research and being open to the possibility that what you find is different than your long-held romantic notions, that were probably jump started by a kids book or television. I have been at this a lot of years and I am still learning. Also, I can look at a modern piece of art or a TV show loosely based in my period, and see the flaws created by the artist or producer who just wanted a flavor, but really did not want to do much research into *real* history. Historical books are popular because the authors have researched artifacts, and excavated trading posts as well as business ledgers or journals. History in that sense comes from a good many sources; and I s'pose for me it is the idea of collecting those little bits and then putting them together to continue building a believable person or character, or setting like a camp."

"That makes sense." Jewel added knodding in agreement. "You mean like this camp?"

"Well, not so much. No insult to the present company but there are a number of things out of place like the sleeping bags and water jugs. They did not exist, for instance, in 1800; same with the plastic bag of coffee, it would have been in a cloth bag and whole bean, and it was common for it to be stored as green coffee beans. As for footwear there were no pointy western boots, instead the boots had square toes and a different cut. There were no wrist watches, instead there were pocket watches. And as for eye-glasses they were made differently. Today our glasses have feet for the bridge of the nose, but back in 1800, for instance, there was a one piece bridge and no feet. Yah, so all those things added together keep reminding me that I am in the 20th century. They're called anachronisms or 'farbs.' As long as they are in view, its hard, if not impossible, to feel like I am in any other time than now. All too often it's because reenactors have not taken the time to rid themselves of things, like a wrist watch, or they just don't care"

"Don't get me wrong, no one here is lazy. It may not be rendezvous, but it's a good camp and I'm having fun. What were doing here is serious business though. As a group we herded up some cattle, got them to the trailers, slaughtered and quartered a steer and now we are camping out, waiting until morning to move the quarters. That steer could just as well be a buffalo, or an elk from a hunt. It could represent one beef slaughtered by an army to feed the soldiery. The armies during the 1700's and early 1800's often had a collection of drovers to herd their beeves. It was their food. This is a real experience, a true experience."

"Wait, wait," interjected Jewel, "Beeves? what is beeves?"

Mark responded, "One beef, two beeves. Well anyways, this is not a period camp, but I am enjoying the camp fire, cooking, skinning, butchering, and it because it is all the same stuff - along with the horses, guns, knives, tomahawks, rifle - my character would have used and handled two hundred years ago."

Jewel had an additional querry, "So, these things that are out of place, you called them anachronisms and farbs?" She paused as she thought, "So...these things bascially ruin the mood or they..." She thought for a moment and raised her hand with her pointer finger extended up, as if to say 'give me a second.' "That stuff kills any chance of experiencing something outside of present day. Is that what I'm hearing?"

"Ya. Pretty much," answered Mark.

"OK, Cantry, was explaining this earlier today but he did it in a different way. Obviously I would not have a 1968 Ford Mustang at a jousting match in the time of the knights. But what you're saying is that there are smaller things that are more ...subtle?" she paused, "I think that's the right word...things that don't stand out as much but can still remind you that it is the 20th century."

"Yep, that's a fair assessment." responded Mark.

"Sounds almost like you are being transported to a different time and place."

"Kind of," Mark said with a nod, "I'll tell you what's really wild, and this has happened to me a half dozen times. When there are no anachronisms, nothing modern intrudes into the setting. Suddenly 'you're there!' Even if for just a few seconds, you feel like you are there, in that time. For instance one of the eight or so rendezvous held at Henry's Fork of the Green River from 1825 to 1840 or Piere's Hole in 1832. It's like being in a "momentary time warp," which isn't a good description because you really haven't changed times, but it's a feeling I think anyone can relate to. It's like icing on the cake to those of us who enjoy this way of life."

"Cantry," she said as she craned her head around, "have you ever had that happen..."

Cantry jumped in, "Well ya. I can think of one time last year when the six of us went on that canoe trip on the Sheyenne. T.J. and I came around the bend and there was Mark and "Z" up on the bank hunting with their muzzleloaders and wearing clothing from the period and it felt like..."

She waited as Cantry paused. She realized he was reliving the moment and she waited for him to continue.

He continued, "It felt like I was watching someone in the Lewis and Clark expedition. It lasted for a few seconds until I saw a metal fence post with a pop-can shot full of holes and that kinda' ripped me back into the present time, but it was really awesome, while it lasted!"

Jewel sat for a bit, in a trance-like state, ruminating on Mark's explantions and description of 'being there,' which some might call a momentary time warp. She also thought about Cantry's explanations earlier that day and saw how much of it fit together, and now this new revelation of his own experience of a significant event. It gave her a greater appreciation for Cantry's passion for history through all the related things over and above muzzleloaders.

She looked up to see G Ray, Ian and Mark moving away from the fire and toward their respective mounts. Cantry leaned over and tapped her on the knee as he knodded toward Sandy.

"Oh, right, the horses," Jewel said as she came out of her pensive mood.

The riders then took some time to brush their horses and give them a drink in the two rubber water buckets they had brought back. The horses did not drink too much as they had all gotten filled up on water from the short water tank on Ian's truck. When all the brushing and watering was done the four came to the fireside.

"Ahhhh, good!" G Ray said with satisfaction in his voice as he let out an air-wash from the bottle of coke. "No loads in the chambers while we sleep, right," he said with authority, "If we have some trouble won't take nothing to cock and aim." To which Mark, Ian, and Cantry all replied affirmatively.

At that point the other four had each picked out a spot under the tarps, horse blankets on the ground and began rolling out their bedrolls their feet nearest the fire-pit. Facing the fire-pit Mark's position was to the far left and to his right was Jewel, then Ian, then Cantry, and on the far right was G Ray.

Ian remarked with a chuckle as he settled in, "I'm going to be what you might call a 'bundling-board' between you two."

Snickers could be heard from Mark and G Ray but no sounds came from either Jewel or Cantry.

After a minute of silence Jewel quietly said, "Thanks for staying out here Mr. Thorvig."

That was quickly followed by, "Yeah, thanks Uncle Ian."

"Your both welcome," replied Ian in a gentle voice.

G Ray, Mark and Cantry each had their respective rifles in hand and laid them parallel to their rolls, with the buttstock near their head and muzzles pointed towards their feet. One by one each person in turn settled into their bedroll and drifted off to sleep, but not before a voice called out, "Goodnight Molly."

Jewel answered, 'Ha-ha, very funny G Ray."

Mark chimed in, "Good night John-Boy."

"I think he's talking to you Cantry," Jewel said facetiously.

Mark quickly responded, "Nah, just wait until he does something really embarrassing. That's when he'll get a good and proper handle."

"Yah, here we go just like the Waltons." Ian remarked.

A short while later, the small talk ended and all was quiet. The night was a peaceful one, slightly chilly, slightly foggy and altogether mosquito-less. The fire of cottonwood, elm and boxelder was no longer flaming and the coals glowed red and cozy warm. What ever meat that had been left over, hung next to the fire and would be eaten in the morning. The rest which had been stuffed into fresh meat bags hung well off the ground and in the morning that meat would be loaded and transported back to Ian's and Barb's farm.

*   *   *

Several miles away the leader of the dogs, cast his copper eyes on a likely chicken coop and approached looking for a way around the fencing. Back and forth he went and then around three of the four corners, but try as he may he could not find a way to get at the chickens inside. As he paced around the coop the chickens scurried to the side opposite the pack leader. Several of the other dogs in the pack, saw this activity of the chickens and tried to approach. The leader was not ready. He turned and flashed his bared teeth and they turned back into the brush at the foot of the shelter belt. The pack had not killed anything in three days and was feeding on the occasional mouse that happened to be in their roaming path.

This homestead was set on the banks of the Sheyenne River

and consisted of a cluster of detached buildings. The farm house, which was not visible from the coop, was occupied. From a single kitchen window, light cast a foot print upon the ground surrounded by the growing darkness. There was no human activity outside and all seemed quiet. The pack leader lifted his nose towards the house, but smelled nothing as the slight breeze was blowing towards the house. Not being able to smell potential danger made him uncomfortable, yet he and the rest of the pack were hungry. The chicken coop seemed like an easy target.

The leader trotted over to the brush where the other dogs waited and he turned around with a short audible panting sound. With this signal, four of the other dogs followed him to the coop. He was hungry as were the others. Their intention before moving-on was as to kill as many chickens as possible and carry them away. As the dogs approached the coop, the chickens moved to the other side of the coop and as they did so the other pack members jumped on the fencing to claw their way through the impediment. The harder the dogs tried to breech the fencing the more the chickens scurried back and forth and began to cackle loudly. The cackling only served to excite the lesser dogs in the pack and with that noise the three other dogs in the brush burst onto the scene and also tried to breech the fencing. They bit at the fence hoping to grab feathers and parts of the chickens and pull something through the voids. Now the dogs also began to bark and growl. The two young shepherds found small voids under the fence and began to dig. In less than a minute one of the two began to yelp loudly and the other dogs stopped to investigate him. He was caught in something. A piece of steel had a grip on his foot and would not let go. The harder he tried to free himself the more it hurt. The Airedale crouched down to help and began to bite at the steel. As the Airedale stood up his head turned to the right. His eyes had caught a movement.

Back at Camp

He began to shift his body to look in the direction of the barn.

Suddenly, a loud boom and the Airedale rolled with a loud yelp and ran towards the shelter belt. The young shepherd looked to the source of the boom and saw only buildings. Several seconds later another boom and the shepherd began to lose consciousness. His life slowly ebbed away as his blood drained onto the freshly dug dirt and grass.

*   *   *

A minute later, the farmer emerged from the corner at the far end of the barn that stood between the coop and the house. He walked up with a flashlight in his hand to view the scene. He could see that the shepherd lay dead. As he cast the flashlight's beam past the corner of the chicken coop, he could see some blood. He followed this to the shelter belt. Taking his time, there was caution in his movements. He used the flashlight to see into all the little nooks and shadows of the brush for any sign of a dog but found none. At this he turned and walked back to the house.

As he entered, he reached for the phone on the wall near the door. "Hey, if anyone's on the line, I need to make a call." Several clicks could be heard on the party-line as the neighbors, whomever they might have been, hung up on their end. He then made the call. If any of the neighbors had remained on the party-line, that would simply mean that word about the pack of dogs would spread faster. "Hello. Hey Howard? Yah, this is Sam. I just shot a shepherd dog at my chicken coop and hit what looked like an Airedale and wounded it. They looked to be heading your way so you might want to go out to check your stock."

The farmer listened and related his encounter to his neighbor. Finally, the call was coming to an end, "Yah. Oh yah. Yah, your welcome. Ok, ok, ok bye now."

*   *   *

Meanwhile, a half mile down the road, the Airedale was trying to reach his hip where a bullet had cut the skin by several inches, but had not hit any muscle or bone. The wound stung noticeably and he tried to stop every few minutes to lick at it. He also needed to keep up with the rest of the pack.

As he reunited with the other dogs who were sitting atop a small rise, he lifted his nose and could smell cattle. All of them were smelling cattle. The incessant bellows both low and high was a sign that the calves had been separated from the cows. It was their rather higher pitched notes that caught the attention of the pack, especially the leader.

Following both their noses and their ears they trotted towards the unsuspecting livestock. Ten minutes of hard trotting and finally the five dogs were in view of the heavy steel fencing of the corral. On one side of the field were the young calves and on the other side of the field next to a building were all the mother-cows. The calves were up-wind of the dogs. The smell of the cattle meant fresh meat if one of them could be brought down.

The pack needed only to cross a dirt road and the intervening ditches. Once they were out of the far ditch, they would be within striking distance of the young cattle. The copper-eyed leader had crossed the road first, bounded the ditch and was now on his approach towards the fencing. Following him each of the other dogs, one by one crossed the road and trotted down into the ditch. Since it was fully dark the pack had the advantage of cover and secrecy. When three dogs were through the ditch, a utility truck pulled out of the nearby farmstead and began to drive up the road towards the crossing where the pack, strung out on either side of the road, laid in wait. The Airedale sat licking his wounds while the other dog, a mixed-black lab, was crouching at the edge of the weeds. As the driver shifted, the grears whined. The sound of the engine grew louder and the truck gained speed. The sound of the engine then fell as another gear was shifted and the sound of the engine became louder and the truck gained speed. All the while it seemed as though the truck would stop when the sound of the engine would suddenly dissapate. Instead of slowing or stopping, the truck continued to gain speed toward the waiting pack.

As soon as the lights of the vehicle shown on the road bed the mixed-lab became anxious to get over the road, but remained in a crouch. Closer and closer came the vehicle. A bright light appeared from the window of the passenger side. From the driver's side an even-brighter light shown from the mechanical spot light built into the roof post just ahead of the wing-window. Its beam pierced the dark and illuminated the area in a broad circle.

As soon as the beam caught the leader's copper eyes, the truck quickly came to a halt. In the leader's experience, vehicles and everything associated with them was bad. He felt the strong beam of light in his eyes. At this occurrence the leader bolted into the darkness. He needed no encouragement as to his next option which was to run for the nearest set of trees, brush and low ground. As he tried to look into the darkness, he saw blue spots. With every blink he saw the dots, but within a minute or so, the blue spots began to dissapate and his night-vision began to increase. The other dogs behind him also followed. At this point the lab also bolted across the road which triggered several doors to open on the truck. Voices shouted back and forth and in the din of human sounds there came a sharp crack, followed by more yelling.

The Airedale had stopped licking his wound and apprehended the truck that now lay directly between the pack and himself. He began to run parallel to the road and, as he did, he ran under a bunch of low lying sand burrs that caught his fur and poked him in the wound on his hip. Surprised, he let out a series of loud yelps and stopped. He spun around to bite at the wound and remove the offending object. It was then he noticed that a light was shining in his direction and several times caught him in the eyes and fouled his night-vision. Suddenly there were shouts. He began to run and could hear the cracks of the several fire-sticks held by the humans. The ground in front of him spit bits of sand and rocks into his face and side, but he continued to run. He was trying to see the road off to his left so he could cross it and as he neared the ditch, he felt the a sting in his shoulder and another in his side. His muzzle dug into the dirt, filling his mouth with moist black soil. After rolling several times he felt weak. He could smell blood; his own. His panting grew heavy as he saw in his mind's eye the sheep that he had helped to kill weeks earlier. As he had watched the sheep bleeding and dying he too was now bleeding and dying. Then all became dark.

Across the field and in the woods leading to a nearby shelter belt the other four dogs found their way through a dense area of blown down trees. Here they rested for a short while. The pangs of hunger, however, were now more persistent than ever. They had been so close to the chickens and now the calves. They had been only yards away from having their bellies full and their hunger sated.

The leader, who was still anxious, had learned to keep moving away from danger. He kept the wind from the farmstead on his left as he moved the remaining pack members over open ground. They continued to move to the east northeast and continued to move until they arrived at a substantial road ditch. They were a bit reluctant to cross and so moved away from it and into the wind which brought them south of another farmstead. Here they paused as the copper-eyed leader wanted to smell the farm and anything that came from it.

All the dogs rested for a while, perhaps several hours or so. It seemed though that the faintest smell of blood and guts was in the wind. It was nothing strong but it was constant. With the light of the new day brightening the landscape, the pack found itself on the move at a trot. Their bellies tight, almost twisted with hunger. Their noses were in the wind; following what they knew was a potential meal. The more they trotted to the northwest the stronger the smell became. But there was also mixed into the smell, the scent of horses, man and fire.

They were now so close that the source of the smell must be only yards away. At this the leader slowed down and allowed the Irish setter and the black lab female to pass him. These would take the vanguard and the leader would flank to the left. The remaining shepherd remained on the right flank. The setter and the lab trotted past some white objects hanging in the trees. Some white walls were on the ground to their left, but they were on the other side of a small ridge. The two could now see the source of the smell, the object of their search, which sat out in the open. A gut pile. It should afford something fresh, something to fill hungry bellies. Never mind the smell of smoke, the smell of horses and people together. Even if it was a quick bite, a couple of pieces, a couple of mouthsfull, just something to eat. There were no buildings and no fences. This was going to be easy; it was open for the taking.

CHAPTER SIX

The Final Encounter

G Ray was up with the first light. He took care of his personal morning routine, followed by Mark and Cantry. The three took turns fanning the surviving coals into a fire with their hats. G Ray, brewed some coffee which he had stuffed in a canvas bag along with a small pot. They munched on leftover meat and the last of the bread. The sky was brightening but the sun had not yet peeked over the horizon when the horses, still at their pickets, became unsettled and spooked. Cantry glanced around to determine the cause of their behavior. Mark and G Ray noticed it as well. As Jewel came to life, she too was turning her head from side to side at which point she quickly scooted forward to pull on her boots and don her jacket.

From under a blanket came Ian's voice, "What the heck's got the horses riled?" and then he too pushed the blanket and sleeping bag away from his face and chest. He looked around with squinting eyes.

"What's wrong with *them*?" Jewel asked Cantry as she nodded her head toward the horses. Her arms were folded as she braced against the cool morning air. Her boots were still cold and she lightly stamped to get the blood moving in her feet.

Cantry, who was standing by the fire pit, at the foot of G Ray's bed and with his back now to Jewel and Mark, raised his hand waist high, motioning the other two behind him to freeze. He lowered himself to his knees as he swore audibly then whispered as he turned around, "Mark, that flinter of yours still loaded?

"All I got to do is prime," whispered back Mark who was still sitting on his bed with his flinter by his side. Mark quickly primed the lock of his rifle. He came to his knees, and began by putting on his belt around his coat, then his shooting pouch and horn then rose up out of the lean-to. Cantry was several feet from his rifle as was G Ray from his own.

"Uncle Ian, if that Forty-four is underneath your saddle, you might want to get it out." Then he loudly whispered," Jewel!"

"Yeah?" Came the reply almost immediately.

"Can you see my Henry?"

G Ray, who had by now moved behind Cantry, quietly interrupted, "I'm already on it lad." Cantry, with his right hand reaching backward, towards G Ray knelt behind the lean-to and grasped the Henry. Cantry slowly, quietly levered a shell into the chamber. He remained in a crouch as he watched Mark ready himself.

Mark felt for his knife and Patterson pistol; making sure they were in their respective places on his belt.

"Dogs?" asked Jewel.

There was nothing to be said just a slow nod from Cantry as he held up two fingers then in a deliberate fashion mouthed the words as he whispered, "I see two of them." As Cantry moved to his left, he could see G Ray manuver to get at his own rifle.

"Shoot straight," whispered G Ray as he also slowly chambered a shell into his Long-Colt Winchester.

Cantry simply nodded without looking at G Ray.

The two dogs were busy pulling apart the gut pile of the recently butchered steer and were not watching as Mark crept out of the east side of the lean-to and Cantry out of the west side. Both remained obscured by the small knoll south of the butcher sight. Meanwhile, G Ray was moving through the horses to a quartering point to the west of the camp and the dogs; just in case they put their nose to the wind and ran. The meat bags hung behind a few feet. Cantry peered through some weeds and short grass. He went to his belly and brought the Henry to his shoulder as he took a bead on one of the wild dogs. It looked like one from his confrontation last summer.

*   *   *

As the copper eyed pack leader approached, he saw movement. It was horses, and humans. He continued to work his way toward the white walled objects on the ground and as he did a human form emerged, head and shoulders and began to mumble. He also heard sounds, like flies, it was a swissp, swissp, swissp, sound coming from the humans as well. The leader was absolutely pinched with hunger. He had been running all night, with nothing to renew his strength. He was ready to fight and take anything that was food. Never mind the other dogs who may find it first, he could always make them back down and then he could eat his fill. But now, he was determined to find and take whatever stuff was the bloody, gutsy, source of the smell; ultimately the source of something that could be eaten.

From his location, the keen nose of the copper-eyed leader immediately picked up more of a meaty smell than of guts. It was a sweet, bloody smell that seemed to emanate from the white objects in the trees. He did not care about the source. He was going to see what these white objects had to offer. If a human got in the way there would be a fight. He could see no buildings, no cars. He could not hear any running engines or smell exhaust in the air. This should be easy. The humans should yell and run. They would, most likely, leave and he would have a meal. If need be, he could chase the humans away. Many times, in the past, he had seen humans with long sticks that ended in shiny spoon shapes, and sticks that had many little sticks in a row which they scraped on the ground. In some instances, the items had been swung at him from a distance but the sticks did not bark or make a loud boom. From his experience, they did not spit the yellow/red flower, they were simply sticks; and the humans that held them would yell and make whining sounds as they ran towards buildings; only, there were no buildings here.

He spied a human moving to stand behind a large tree. This human had what seemed to be one of those long sticks that had an odd spoon shape on the end and the human was holding it backwards. Here again, he knew the stick would be waived at him, this frail human would stand behind the tree and just waive a stick at him. The tree presented no barrier. As the leader of this pack, he would growl and menace and the stick wielding human should run away, maybe drop the stick too. Even if the human stood a long-ways off, he could ignore the human and use his keen nose to find the source of the meat smell and then eat. The copper eyed leader thought to himself, "Move away humans or I will attack you. Run away or I will bite you, rip, tear and bite you again."

*   *   *

Just then, Mark, who was to Cantry's right, was slowly standing to hide behind a large cottonwood tree, turned his head. He had heard the sound of swishing grass and as he turned, he was confronted by a snarling shepherd cross, a mere twenty-five yards away, its piercing copper eyes trained on Mark, its hackles were raised and teeth bared.

"We got company," whispered Mark gently.

"You're kidding," Cantry mumbled under his breath. After which he did not utter a further sound, he was already committed to the task of silently getting into position where he could bring the Henry to bear on the two wild dogs at the gut pile.

Mark slowly pivoted on the ball of one foot. He avoided eye-contact with the snarling shepherd, but kept the form in his periphery. With the muzzle pointed down, he brought the rifle around as well. The dog stood stiff legged, still growling. With every movement that Mark made, the growling rose in intensity as if to say, "Move away, move away!" Mark positioned himself until he could begin to raise the rifle. He almost had a bead on the chest of the feral animal. Suddenly it bolted toward him!

With the lock on full cock, he quickly pulled the set trigger and instinctively brought his finger to bear on the front trigger. As his sights came in line with the lunging beast, he held his breath and touched the front trigger. The rifle boomed.

Mark lost sight of the animal through the cloud of smoke, only to realize the black mass of fur was still in motion. Instantly he switched the rifle to his left hand as his right hand jerked the Paterson out of its holster. With two quick thumb pulls, Mark shot twice at the mass of fur. He cocked a third time ready for another shot at the writhing, growling animal.

Ian's voice erupted, "Mark! He's down! Get back!" Ian now rose up to a stoop, one hand on the ground with his revolver drawn and at full cock. He did not dare shoot as the dog was too close to Mark.

Even though Cantry knew the rifle was to be fired, he still lurched a bit. The two dogs jerked their heads up from the greasy viands. Cantry quickly reacquired his target on the chest of the skinny Irish Setter, and fired. The running mate jerked its head to the left as he watched his companion flop backward to the ground. The lab attempted to vacate the scene to the west, but it was too late. Cantry had just levered in another shell and took a bead for a running shot. As he pulled the trigger, he heard, on his far left, the boom of G Ray's 45 Long-Colt. He saw the lab tumble. Cantry levered another shell and swung back to his first dog. It was still motionless. Though Cantry knew he had fired several shots, he was oblivious to the fact that Mark had shot twice more. When he stood and turned towards Mark, he let out a gasp. He could see that a large black shepherd lay dead several feet from Mark's position.

*   *   *

The copper-eyed leader, as quick as a flash of lightening, sprang forward and was ready to begin to fight or chase. He had almost reached the first human and was ready to snap, fight and bite, when the human with the stick was suddenly obscured by white smoke. The leader was struck by something that pushed at him violently sending his right shoulder to the ground. Now he could feel his body tumble forward in an awkward twisting motion. He tried to regain his balance, but he could only roll. He bit at the object that had struck him, but found nothing. As he tried to rise, he saw two more puffs of smoke and heard two sharp cracks and felt a sting in his side and another in his back. He tried to bite. Things seemed to be moving in slow motion. He tried to take a breath. It felt like he had water in his throat, but when he exhaled out came blood. He rolled to his side and viewed the blood on the grass, it was his own blood. How could that be? What had bitten him? As he tried to rise, his back legs pushed and kicked. His front paws, with claws extended, pulled at the ground, but he could not rise. The light was fading along with his energy. The sounds around him became more distant. He lay his head on the ground and with one last convulsion his lungs exhaled. All became black.

*   *   *

Mark, kept the Paterson pointed at the copper-eyed shepherd ready for a third shot. He took several deep breaths trying to calm himself. His heart was racing. He did not dare turn toward Cantry. Without taking his eyes off of the animal he exhaled loudly, then called out to Cantry, "Well, what happened?"

"I think their both done." Came the words quickly and confidently. He watched Mark, whose arm was outstretched holding his pistol and breathing heavily. Cantry also held his rifle in the same direction as he took small steps to Mark's left and past the tree.

"Okay! I think this one's down too." Mark exclaimed.

"I'm on him," Cantry assured Mark. "Step back and get that rifle reloaded." Cantry studied the scene. "Wow! That's close!"

"Yah, move back Mark, I'm on him too," called out Ian who, by now, was standing with his pistol, still at full cock, braced on top of the corner pole by Mark's bed. The barrel was also pointing at the lifeless body that had been the bold, vicious copper-eyed leader.

Mark rotated the cylinder of the Patterson to a neutral position, holstered it and turned his attention to the .54 flintlock. Forty seconds later he was loaded and then gave a few taps from the horn for prime and closed the frizzen over the pan. Mark now took the initiative directed at Cantry, "Okay, cowboy, you'd better refill too."

Cantry reached into his vest pocket where he could feel four more shells and replaced the two shots he had made. At that point everyone froze in place. All heads were slowly turning from side to side to listen for anymore sounds but there were no more. There seemed at that point a sort-of "collective sigh" from the three as the fast action was over. Nothing else seemed to be moving. There was nothing, but a slight breeze and the new-leaves fluttering in response. Their quiet little camp, which had quickly become a shootout, was once again settled.

Just then Jewel yelled out excitedly, "GUYS! There goes one more!" As she stepped back from the trees and pointed at the newly discovered threat.

Cantry reacted by running around the cluster of trees to try and get a shot at the fleeing beast. Try as he might, he was unable to draw a bead due to the undulating terrain and varying clumps of short and tall weeds. The dog was running back in the direction of yesterday's herd drive. Cantry emitted several epithets at the missed chance. The three watched another rather large shepherd cross, get away without so much as a scratch. It ran until it reached a knoll and stopped for just a second. It turned to look back at the camp where its compatriots now lay dead. The fourth dog then resumed its escape. Cantry caught several glimpses of it as it ran up and over another knoll. For a second Cantry looked at his horse and considered going after the fleeing dog.

Mark saw his reaction and quipped, "you'd never catch up to it. By the time you get the bridle on…" His sentence trailed off as he slowly shook his head.

Cantry sighed as he knew to go after the animal would be an exercise in futility. "Well, let's first go check out the two from the gut pile, just to make sure their done with."

Mark spoke up quickly and a little shaky, "I think I can say that mine's definitely down!"

After checking the three dead dogs, they returned to the camp fire ready to sit down when Mark looked around and asked, "Hey, where's G Ray?" The words were no sooner out of his mouth when a 'ka-boooom' emanated from the direction of the fourth dog. But the shot was quite far away. Although the dog was gone; all three now focused their attention in that general direction.

Just then Mark felt a nudge from Ian who nodded at the picket line. Mark looked at the picket line and said incredulously, "and where's Abigail?" followed by a long exasperated grunt.

"You don't s'pose that G Ray somehow took…Do you?"

"Well I don't know who else it would be," replied Ian as he turned to Mark and with a joking sort of call to his voice said, "Abby was tied near to mine. I'll bet that Winger reached over just far enough down the picket and worked on Abby's lead rope because the horse and lead rope are both missing."

"That little…!" Mark did not finish the thought. He stood there with his left hand at his side, the right still holding the rifle.

"Well, shouldn't we go see who it is?" queried Cantry.

"N-n-n-nope," answered Ian. "Before we all go running out in that direction, we don't even know where he is. I have no doubt it's G Ray. He's probably trying to get at that fourth dog. I'd just as soon stay back in this area to check on the horse's ropes. If you want to, take your Henry." He paused a bit as he looked out at the horizon, "Maybe you and Mark could at least go to the knoll where you last saw G Ray. Take a gander and see if you can spot him or Abby. Besides, if he needs us he'll probably whistle or something."

Cantry nodded his assent at the wisdom of Uncle Ian's statement.

"Huh, with all this excitement I might have to take a leak," said Ian jokingly, then he followed with, "I'll be right back."

"Yep, me too," Jewel said quickly, "That's not a bad idea."

"You go ahead Jewel, I'll wait till you get back." Ian suggested as he sat down.

"Okay, be right back." Jewel said as she began to walk away from camp at a quick pace.

With that Cantry and Mark trotted over to the knoll where they had last seen G Ray, hoping to locate him. They stood watch for quite a while, searching the horizon, waiting to see something, anything moving out in the distance. By the time they turned around they saw Jewel back at the fire.

"Coffee's ready," came Jewel's voice loudly.

"That was quick," replied Cantry.

Mark and Cantry looked at each other, then at the fire and nodded. Coffee sounded really good to the two men. Each took one more quick look out into the distance, then headed back to the fire.

Back at the fire ring, Mark confided, "I'm so pumped up on adrenaline right now, I probably don't need any coffee…but I'll take some anyway." He emitted a short laugh.

Jewel looked at Mark in agreement and added in a shakey voice, "I'm still pretty excited too. You guys might as well fill your own cups, I'm way too shaky to pour without spilling or even take a sip. Hey, Cantry you should tell Mark about Curty and his shot."

Cantry nodded his head as he looked at Mark, "Yep, you'll appreciate that one. I'll tell you about it in a little bit."

Ian, who was finally returning from his own "visit to the bushes" was visibly shaking his head as he walked and exclaimed, "I never fired a shot. I never fired a shot."

Mark, who had not filled his cup yet, turned to look at Ian, "Yeah, but you had my back," he reassured, "and that's worth a lot, shot or no shot. Yah know, maybe I should go look for Abby right now."

Taking up the coffee kettle from Cantry, Ian poured some fresh hot coffee for Mark and in turn for himself. Immediately he thrust the cup at Mark who took the cup.

Mark looked down at the steam lifting from the coffee and paused for a second. "Well," Mark said as his eyes darted to Ian's, "I guess a cup won't hurt." With coffee in hand, he walked over to the high-line to look at the spot where Abby should have been tied.

Cantry and Ian remained seated at the fire and waited for the coffee to cool a bit before placing the rims of the metal cups to their lips. A short while later, there were several "ahhh's" as the coffee was sipped and then quaffed down. Shortly thereafter, each person began to talk about the morning's events. Jewel, after taking several deep breaths, and exhaling loudly, poured a cup for herself with a minimum of shaking, then placed the small kettle next to the coals.

Each person had their version of those few tense minutes and what each had done to cover the other's back. Finally, Mark returned from the high-line to join in. He spoke about how Cantry had readied himself, then Cantry would pick up from there and add a bit from his perspective, then Mark again, and then Ian. Jewel added what she saw or heard and on and on it went as each person's story dovetailed into the other three.

After a short time, Cantry was down to the last gulp of his coffee and stood up. As he looked down, he saw Jewel's countenance change. She also stood up to look around him and across the open grass and trees. Cantry turned around, stooped to one knee to look under the trees and back at the far knoll. There in the distance, emerged G Ray; clearly recognizable by his white zip-up chaps and the .45 Long-Colt he carried in his hand. Thankfully Mark's horse, Abigail, was being led back by G Ray.

Jewel remarked, "Well, Mark, I guess you don't have ta' go lookin' for your horse. And what does he…What's he wearing? Mark that looks like your vest."

"Yep," He borrowed my waiscoat last night for padding, so I guess he put it on this morning when the dog action happened."

Jewel remarked in a soft tone, "Boy do I feel out of place. Everyone's wearing some sort of old clothing or using an old gun or something, except for me."

Cantry jumped in, "Well, get with the program…Molly."

"Hey, who told who about the blackpowder shoot?" she retorted. Cantry said nothing. Mark grinned at Cantry but said nothing as well. The four watched G Ray as he came in whistling. He stopped and thrust his rifle into the air. Then he grabbed a hand-full of mane and thrust his right leg over the horse's back and rode in.

"You got em?" called out Cantry.

G Ray, in response held up his hand with a "thumbs-up" sign. At which point all who were there at the side of the fire whistled and cheered, and soon the horses were whinnying back and forth as well.

Jewel turned from the focus of their attention, poured the remaining coffee into an available cup and addressed the group, "I'll get boiling, some water for more coffee."

G Ray rode in and dismounted. He related his narrative of the events just past. After shooting the one dog he noticed that Mark's horse was on the next opening to the west and walking away from the commotion, but still feeding. He jogged over to Abby, which he jokingly referred to as "Abby-Normal," in an attempt to catch her. She wasn't too sure of him at first, but she stopped long enough for a sniff. Then G Ray related that he heard Jewel shout something and he could not make out what it was. He looked out in the open, up wind of course, and saw a dog running. Then G Ray came alive in his narrative.

"Well then I says to myself, I can't let no mongrel get loose wit'out me havin' a poke at him. So, I quick took the lead rope wrapped up a half-hitch around ole Abby-Normal's muzzle, t'rew my leg over and lit out after that dog. Jeepers could he run!"

"Well," he paused to take a breath, "that dog was so busy lookin' back at you folks that he never seen me until it was too late. I jumped off that horse while it was still walking, came up from behind a knoll and as soon as that dog saw the horse he stopped. That's when I got him. At thirty yards! He couldn't smell me, 'cause I came up cross wind of him and he never heard the horse running out in the open. After I shot the dog it was time to go get the mare again and I was so far from camp that walkin' back wit' my gun would be just as far. Tha'twas no farther than going after the horse, so I trotted after Abby-Normal, and caught her again after she smelled your vest, of course."

"WES-kit," replied Mark as he supplied the necessary moniker, "it's called a weskit, but it's spelled, w-a-i-s-t-c-o-a-t" [17]

Then G Ray began again, "Oh yah, so I got ahold of Abby-Normal and came in here. When I stopped to check the half-hitch, that's when you folks seen me." He paused for a moment as Jewel handed a cup of coffee to him. "Say, looks like some gooood coffee."

"Yep!" Jewel began as she looked at Mark, "I think I'm done shaking."

G Ray who did not miss a beat interjected in a humorous tone, "What was the deal? D'you get excited in all the action? Maybe a little "buck-fever, huh." He winked at Jewel. As he lifted his cup, he remarked with his heavy Norwegian brogue. "Thanks Molly. Well, skoal!"

Jewel simply shook her head as she put the small pot near the coals. She was correct about the new nick-name. It stuck like glue. No, she did not have any historic clothes or guns or anything but she did have a rather historic "handle."

The five sat down at the fireside for some time and drank coffee, as they told and retold the events of the morning. Soon the coffee was polished off and the rest of the cooked meat was collected for the trail snacks. The lean-to was pulled apart and the pieces of canvas used to double wrap some of the meat to further protect it and staunch any blood, in the cheese cloth, from getting on the saddles. The group assembled and began their ride out to where Barb would meet them with the truck and trailer. G Ray's horse, Butternut, and Cantry's Horse, Storm were used as a pack horses for the rest of the meat that no one else could take as well as the horse gear like water buckets. G Ray and Cantry each walked their mounts as they headed west. Ian dragged the rolled-up steer hide using one of the long ropes.

*   *   *

It had been and eventful two days. The chain of events never would have been imagined by Cantry and Jewel, or, anyone else for that matter. Not only did they take it all in stride but each was a bit sorry the whole ordeal was over. Their ride onto and into the open spaces of the prairie and grasslands would be a story they would remember for the rest of their lives.

Jewel and Mark who were in front of the caravan, turned to ride back to Cantry and G Ray. Cantry voiced his thoughts as the two rode up. "When we took a ride looking for strays, I ah, never would'a guessed that there would be so much goin' on" He paused for a moment, "I'll never look at a dog the same way again, when it's running out in the open. Some of this turned out to be kind of a fun deal...we could almost, or ought to do some parts of it again."

Jewel, piped in from the other side of Cantry, "Yah? Which parts?"

Mark snickered and added, "No doubt." as he shook his head. He looked down at Cantry and pointed the conversation to the upcoming rendezvous and getting a camp set up yet this week. Cantry smiled at the thought as he tugged on the reins to coax Storm along.

With two riders walking, the party and their horses slowly made their way west. A little further down the trail would bring them within sight of the vehicle waiting for them on the other side of the coulee. Each person in his or her own way, reflected on the expanse of their surroundings and understood their blessings that in this modern day and age they could still chase cattle, do a little shooting, and camp "on-the-spot."

Ride in the Open Spaces

*   *   *

As Jewel viewed the trail she was momentarily lost in the events of the last two days. She considered what she would say to people in a way that would capture all the excitement and range of emotions. She thought about the ride, the killed calf, the injured dog, the butchering and the camp, and the relentless, bloody wild dogs; and in that moment she had an epifany. She could envision how a number of people would react. They would begin by asking, *"But wouldn't it just be easier if you guys would have..."*

She now understood more deeply what Cantry was trying to convey to her the day before about historical camping and performing activities. Yes, she could have read it in a book, but her personal, hands-on experience made it all so much more relevant, so much more real. However; the best part was, like her own pioneer ancestors who came to this area almost a hundred years before her, she and her modern band of friends and neighbors could still roam relatively unhindered, encountering some of the same dangers as the pioneers.

She watched from the back of the string as Mark caught up to Ian, who rode in the lead followed by Cantry and G Ray walking their mounts. Not only could they still roam, they did roam.

Just then, she felt like she was really back in the days of the early pioneers. Everything around her seemed like a different time period; including her being in it. While Jewel was revelling in the sudden "time warp," she looked up and saw the truck. It was not anything bad necessarily, but she was snapped back into modern times. The sensation was fleeting, to say the least.

She had never experienced anything like it before. Maybe it was what someone from 1840 or 1850 would have seen, heard, smelled or tasted. It touched her deeply and was as much apart of the last several days as the rythm of Sandy's gate. She wanted to prolong the time warp; to get back that feeling somehow, but her mental efforts to feel it again were in vain. There were too many modern intrusions. She tried to block the truck from her thoughts, but found her mind fixated on "not seeing" the truck.

She quickly realized that her experience was not a feeling that could come from something being intentionally orchestrated, or un-thinking a thought. Rather, her conciousness had been captured by the whole setting, and transported to another time; if only for a couple of seconds. Just as quickly it was gone, but she had felt it and it enlivened her. Seeing the truck was like walking through a one-way-door. Its modern shape had just killed any chance of reconnecting with the time warp.

On the other hand, it startled her a bit to think this had all happened because she and Cantry were just doing a job that cattle folks had been doing for years; as a part of their every day life. They had basically gone on a cattle round-up. Throw in a couple of encounters with wild dogs and an over-night under the stars, roasted beef at the fire with friends and last but not least the history-lessons, and it became much more than the sum of its parts. It had turned into an adventure like no other.

She played the whole scenario over and over in her mind. She kept coming back to the general idea that history really had made an impact on her, and all who had been a part of the events of the last several days. She had to admit it saddened her to think the adventure was over, and yet, she felt so blessed as she looked at Cantry realized her grand opportunity to share this time with him. It meant everything to her. It had all started so simply. In the larger picture, everyone in the group now had a common history; a shared experience that would create a bond for many years to come.

*　　　　*　　　　*

Cantry stopped for a second to look back at Jewel and could see that she was deep in thought. He turned to address her. "What's up? You look like you're thinking mighty hard. You sad or what?

Jewel looked at Cantry and smiled. "No. Well, maybe a little sad. Actually, I feel blessed. Your talk yesterday, and Mark's too, about history is really coming to roost, especially the part about blending into the experience, or be woven into it. I think I'd like to give this rendezvous camping some serious effort."

Now it was Cantry who was knitting his brow.

She then offered, "if you're wondering about my sudden interest, I'll have to tell you and Mark about what I just encountered. A feeling about being on the trail with all of you; but first, let's get loaded up. When there's no distractions, I'll tell you all about it."

"Well, Uncle Ian says that inspiration can come from the strangest of places."

Jewel, with a smile, tilted her head sideways. Scanning the near-cloudless sky, she thoughtfully replied, "Yeah, who knew that wild-dogs, chasing cattle, would lead us into this adventure."

"Yah sure, it was supposed to be just a um..." Cantry thought for a moment as he peered up at Jewel. A smile slowly formed as he turned to face Jewel directly; then he finished the thought, "a ride in the open spaces."

finis

Author's Note

As a youngster working on the family farm in eastern North Dakota, I would go on errands and car-rides with my Grandfather, Marty Kruse. We would drive between the lake cottage on Prairie Lake, near Pelican Rapids, MN and the farm, north of Kindred, ND, remarking on deer and duck habitat; we judged the condition of farm fields and met farmers in the course of their chores. It was during these car rides he would relate to me a number of hunting and trapping stories from his youth in Iowa, from early adulthood in Minnesota and from the start of his farming career in North Dakota. He referenced incidents from the 1930's up through the 1960's in which he shot or chased, the occasional dog that had slunk into the barnyard and killed chickens or molested the other livestock. My grandfather was defending his homestead against interlopers. He did not harbor any particular harshness against dogs. Rather, he himself had owned and used dogs for hunting waterfowl and upland game. He loved to watch them work the terrain, especially prairie chickens before the laws prohibited the use of dogs for that game. He was also an excellent judge of horseflesh and treated his animals and livestock respectfully. However, problem strays could not be tolerated by him or other farmers.

During the 1970's and through the 1980's, running dogs and wild dogs had become a significant problem in Eastern North Dakota and Western Minnesota. These dogs actually formed into a number of packs. In some instances, farm dogs were lured in as a part of a pack, or in trying to defend the farm yard, they met their fate as they were overwhelmed by a pack.

The incident regarding, Curtis "Curty" Vangsness, shooting a dog only feet from the vehicle, really happened. He and his brother Sinster, were known for their shooting skills. If Curty had hesitated, he would have been maimed or killed. Those dogs, which roamed near Kindred N.D. and surrounding communities, seemed to have little fear of man, became quite bold and presented a real and present danger.

As I look at the outdoor news (2019) there are, and have been for several years, weekly encounters with wolves, coyotes, mountain lions, and roaming dogs. These encounters have occurred in suburbs and even in the middle of large cities! Any of these wild or feral animals can threaten our pets, livestock and family, especially our little children; right in "our own back-yard." Coyotes have proven to be the worst offenders in suburbs/cities and have been caught on camera attacking children, seriously injuring people and killing pets. Cougars have been the worst offenders along rural hiking/biking trails, especially in Colorado, and have been responsible for attacking, maiming and killing runners and bikers. This is not a "call to arms" to wipe out these animals. However, since their habitat overlaps with ours, it is a reminder to be vigilant in the protection of our families, ourselves, our homes and neighborhoods. We should ever be aware of our surroundings. We are the defenders of our hearth and home, our children and family.

As an aside, in 1977, the brothers, Curtis and Sinster Vangsness, introduced me to black powder shooting while my brother, Bob, my Uncle George Kruse and I were out at the Vangsness family farm along the banks of the Sheyenne River. We were enjoying a day of shooting our rifles and other sundry firearms. In the course of the day, Curty n' Sinster, (their names were often said as one word in much the same way we say "Lewis and Clark"), revealed a new acquisition in the form of an original .58 caliber Zouave rifle; a military muzzleloader. After they had loaded it and shot it, I just had to have a try for myself. I ended up shooting the Zouave as much or more than my new, high-powered rifle, which I had brought with me to sight-in.

With that first shot from an original 19th century muzzle-loader, I was hooked; I just did not know it at the time. What started as a simple trigger pull, eventually lead to a my purchase of a .54 caliber Thompson/Center "Hawken" rifle (in kit form) in 1983. That purchase, in turn, gave birth to a fulfilling lifestyle, the central theme of which has been, attention to and the historical use of...muzzleloaders, especially flintlocks. What started as a spark, has become a flame.

John W. Hayes, Author

End Notes

1. **CRP** stands for Conservation Reserve Program. This is a government program which encourages farmers to leave a portion of their farmed acres idle or out of production. By doing so, the farmer receives a government subsidy. In this case the land is not tilled and grows grass and weeds; even brush which creates habitat for game.

2. **National Grasslands** are Federal lands consisting of "prairie-pothole" and set aside as natural areas similar in use and scope to National Forests.

3. **Metis** (pronounced MAY-tee) referrs to a person of mixed descent especially in Canada; a person with one white parent and one American Indian parent. Many, being buffalo hunters and trappers, were seen during the early nineteenth century following the trading routes from St. Paul, to Moorhead, Minnesota, then to Pembina, North Dakota and up to Winnipeg. They roamed up and down the Red River Valley following the buffalo and spread throughout North Dakota and Manitoba westward in their pursuits.

4. Artist **Alfred Jacob Miller** painted and sketched the people of the frontier especially the hunters and trappers. In several of his pieces the men are wearing spurs on their moccasins.

5. In 1836 **Samuel Colt** invented a five-shot .36 caliber revolver with a retractable trigger and no trigger guard. It utilized percussion cap ignition.

6. **Capote** (pronounced: ka-POE) is a coat made from a wool tradeblanket. Seventy percent of the blankets traded prior to 1802 were White colored English or White colored French Blankets. Often capotes were made of heavy wool duffel. Generally capotes have hoods and many were taylored. Other capotes were made like a box-frock with an open front. During the 17th 18th and 19th centuries there were many woolen mills in England and France.

The wool blankets of the 20 century commonly came from British mills owned by Hudson's Bay as well as Early Witney and Sons of Oxfordshire, England; which mills are renown for having produced, among other colors, the scarlet (by Hudson's Bay and Witney) and emerald green (by Witney).

7. **FFg** is a designation for the size of black powder grains. It is derived from a screen with 24 wires per inch that is used to separate and grade dry black powder. "F" stands for "fine" and "g" stands for "grain." The screen allows smaller granules to pass but retains the larger ones. Shooters simply refer to it as "double F." Generally, FFg is considered rifle powder for .54 caliber and larger as well as powder for larger long-guns and fowling pieces. Other designations for black powder are:

Fg (one F) is generally used for small canon but also large bore guns like .80 and .90 caliber.

FFFg (three F) is used for pistols and smaller bore rifles, .45 caliber and smaller.

FFFFg (four F) is used for priming a flintlock.

8. A **touch hole** is a small hole or vent in the side of the barrel which is situated above the priming pan of the lock. The size of the hole is generally less than 5/64 in diameter. The powder flash in the pan of the lock, pushes through the touch hole and ignites the powder inside the breech end of the barrel.

9. A **set trigger**, often referred to as a double-set trigger is an additional trigger, used to convert the pull of the main trigger into a "hair trigger" and is done for purposes of accuracy.

10. **Spoke and Honda** are parts of a lariat. The honda is the small loop at one end through which the lariat is threaded to create the loop for lassoing. The spoke is the short length of the lariat outside the honda which is not a part of the loop.

11. Running water through grey ashes, and filtering the liquid

produces lye, a necessary ingredient in basic soap making. Wetting a handfull of powdery ash and rubbing it on the hands or any surface, will lift and clean the oils and grease.

12. **Char cloth** is natural cloth that has been charred but kept from burning completely. The fabric is generally made of cotton, linen, or other 100 percent natural plant fiber. Neither wool nor synthetics are used. The charring process is generally accomplished by putting the natural cloth into a sealable can, with a tiny air hole. It is placed in a fire and allowed to smoke. When the smoke lessens the can is removed, the hole is plugged and the can is allowed to cool a good half an hour. Due to the lack of oxygen the cloth is charred but not burnt. It will catch a spark and begin to glow hot.

13. **Linen tow** is the shorter linen fibers and bark that are left-overs from cleaning broken flax stalks and leaving the long fibers better suited for spinning good thread.

14. **Patching** is a piece of cloth that envelopes the round ball, and helps secure it in the barrel and keeps the projectile firmly against the powder. Patching is often made from pillow ticking or some sort of dense linen fabric which averages about .12 thousandths of an inch thick.

15. Spit is often used to lubricate a patch. Different oils and rendered tallow are also used to lube a patch and help in loading and reloading.

16. The term "**all the way home**" means that the projectile is pushed all the way to and firmly tamped down against the powder at the breech end of the barrel.

17. A **waistcoat** (pronounced WES-kit) can be either sleeveless or sleeved. During the eighteenth century It was generally worn over the shirt as a minimum amount of clothing to be considered "nearly dressed." In this story Mark's waistcoat is sleeveless. During the eighteenth century this garment was not called a vest.